Praise for *Where the Wild Ladies Are*

One of BBC Culture's Best Books of the Year

"*Where the Wild Ladies Are* immediately became one of my favorite story collections. The ghosts have got the numbers on us, as Matsuda knows, and it's a joy to see the living and the dead by the light of her radiant imagination. At once playful, joyful, and radically subversive." —KAREN RUSSELL, author of *Orange World and Other Stories*

"Aoko Matsuda's feverish mashups of the civilized and the wild, the mythological and the modern, are daringly strange and hauntingly funny. Her stories burrow into a subterranean place in the psyche where dreams, fairy tales, and ghost stories mingle in a raucous, beguiling party that I wished I never had to leave." —ALEXANDRA KLEEMAN, author of *Intimations*

"Aoko Matsuda's delightful ghosts have all the characteristics of people you know: they could be your dear friends, judgmental relatives, casually encountered busybodies who seem to have too much time on their hands. As you progress through the stories in *Where the Wild Ladies Are*, Matsuda ties together strands and characters so that the book as a whole feels even richer and deeper than you first thought."

—KELLY LINK, author of *Get in Trouble*

"In these absorbing stories, Matsuda animates ancient tales with a humor and resonance that will be thrilling to the modern reader. But she goes beyond even that; she suffuses them with heart, making them her very own. For fans of fabulist fiction, this is as good as it gets." —AMELIA GRAY, author of *Gutshot*

"In death, Matsuda's wild ladies are able to doff society's shit to get up to mirthful hi-jinks. Hanging the grotesque next to the quotidian, fun next to fable, this is a book of startling beauty and insight. You will want to read these stories again and again."

—MARIE-HELENE BERTINO, author of *Parakeet*

"Matsuda's *Where the Wild Ladies Are* is a collection of interconnected, slightly spooky feminist retellings of Japanese folktales . . . Matsuda punctures the folktale serenity and brings us into the now through references to the cruelties of global capitalism and western cultural hegemony." —JULIA IRION MARTINS, *Full Stop*

"[Matsuda] has a light but lasting touch . . . A delightful, daring collection." —*Kirkus Reviews*

"These ghosts are not the monstrous, vengeful spirits of the original stories; they are real people with agency and personalities, finally freed from the restraints placed on living women. Funny, beautiful, surreal and relatable, this is a phenomenal book." —*The Guardian*

"In this enjoyable and enigmatic collection of short stories, Aoko Matsuda retells traditional Japanese ghost stories with a contemporary, feminist slant. The many female ghosts that crop up so often in old Japanese tales appear in many guises here—as forceful saleswomen, or a cynical aunt lecturing her niece about slavishly following fads. They're smart and formally inventive: one story is a self-help column, while a series of stories revolve around the strange goings on at Mr Tei's incense factory. Beauty, jealousy and women's place in Japanese society are all explored in stories which are funny, strange and intriguing." —*Tatler*

"Taking a collection of traditional Japanese ghost stories and crafting them into often humorous yet painfully relevant tales is a move of pure genius by Aoko

Matsuda. Taking place in a contemporary setting, with a decidedly feminist bend, *Where the Wild Ladies Are* takes classic Japanese ghost stories—which make up some of the best in the world—and rewrites them to make them relevant to the current gender climate of modern-day Japan. Witty, biting, and poignant, Matsuda's collection is a pleasantly haunting surprise." —JESSICA ESA, *Metropolis*

"This was an amazing read. A troupe of women are sent in from another world in order to help relieve the angst of the people in this world."

—HIROKO KITAMURA, *Hon no zasshi sha*

"Turning one's back on despair and instead channeling all one's energy into living as one's true self is what gives one the strength to take on spectral form. This is a call to power to live with sufficient conviction to become ghosts." —AKIKO OHTAKE, *Asahi Shimbun*

"An enjoyable and satisfying read, coming out of a sense of discomfort and unease around gender inequality. This is a short story collection where classic works from rakugo and kabuki are developed in the author's unique style." —ASAYO TAKII, *Nami*

WHERE THE WILD LADIES ARE

WHERE THE WILD LADIES ARE

AOKO MATSUDA

TRANSLATED FROM THE JAPANESE BY POLLY BARTON

SOFT SKULL  NEW YORK

Library of Congress Cataloging-in-Publication Data
Names: Matsuda, Aoko, 1979– author. | Barton, Polly (Translator), translator.
Title: Where the wild ladies are / Aoko Matsuda ; translated from the Japanese by Polly Barton.
Other titles: Obachantachi no iru tokoro. English
Description: First Soft Skull edition. | New York : Soft Skull Press, 2020.
Identifiers: LCCN 2020017381 | ISBN 9781593766900 (paperback) | ISBN 9781593766917 (ebook)
Subjects: LCSH: Matsuda, Aoko, 1979– —Translations into English.
Classification: LCC PL873.A86 O3313 2020 | DDC 895.63/6—dc23
LC record available at https://lccn.loc.gov/2020017381

Cover design & Soft Skull art direction by salu.io
Book design by Wah-Ming Chang

Published by Soft Skull Press
1140 Broadway, Suite 704
New York, NY 10001
www.softskull.com

Printed in the United States of America
7 9 10 8

Contents

Note

The stories in this collection draw inspiration from traditional Japanese ghost and yōkai tales, many of which have been immortalized as kabuki or rakugo performances. A complete list of references and brief outlines of the original works can be found on page 255.

WHERE THE WILD LADIES ARE

Smartening Up

I am a beautiful woman.
I am a beautiful, intelligent woman.
I am a beautiful, intelligent, sexy
    woman.
I am a beautiful, intelligent, sexy,
    caring woman. I am—

"Okay, that's the right side done. I'll start on the left now." From just beside my ear, the beautician's voice cut through the affirmations with which I was busy filling up every inch of my headspace.

"Sure, thanks," I responded automatically.

The woman adjusted the towel draped over my chest, then moved to stand on my left. She pressed some buttons on the machine, and it beeped twice—*beep, beep.* Thinking it wouldn't do to stare too intently, I directed my eyes up at the ceiling. Soon enough, I began to feel a faint, tingling pain traversing my arm. This level of pain I was totally fine with. The machine beeped again—*beep, beep.*

> *I am a beautiful, intelligent, sexy,*
> *   caring woman with a fantastic dress*
> *   sense.*
> *I am a beautiful, intelligent, sexy,*
> *   caring woman with a fantastic dress*
> *   sense and unique taste in furniture*
> *   and accessories.*
> *I am a beautiful, intelligent, sexy,*
> *   caring woman with a fantastic dress*
> *   sense and unique taste in furniture*
> *   and accessories, and I'm a superb*
> *   cook to boot.*

In time with the rhythmic beep-beeping of the machine, I went on adding to my list of qualifications.

Like a line of cans moving down a factory conveyor belt, my future assets flowed past me in a steady stream, offering the promise of a new me.

I am a beautiful, intelligent, sexy, caring woman with a fantastic dress sense and unique taste in furniture and accessories, and I'm a superb cook to boot, who sometimes rustles up delicious cakes and sweets in no time at all.

Beep, beep. Beep, beep.

I am a beautiful, intelligent, sexy, caring woman with a fantastic dress sense and unique taste in furniture and accessories, and I'm a superb cook to boot, who sometimes rustles up delicious cakes and sweets in no time at all, and everybody loves me the moment they meet me.

Beep. Beep. Beep. Beep.

I am a beautiful, intelligent, sexy,
caring woman with a fantastic dress
sense and unique taste in furniture
and accessories, and I'm a superb
cook to boot, who sometimes rustles
up delicious cakes and sweets in
no time at all, and everybody loves
me the moment they meet me, and
my skin is so soft and smooth that
people just want to reach out and
touch it.

I am—

"Right, you're all done! I'm going to cool it off for you, so don't move just yet."

The beautician's slightly dated makeup was immaculately applied, her beige-slicked lips thin as an archer's bow. She parted them now to smile broadly at me. A saying that I'd read or heard somewhere came back to me: "You can change your destiny simply by lifting the corners of your mouth. Good fortune comes spilling out of every smile." The beautician had perfect teeth, I thought, and this set my eyes wandering, processing every detail of the open-plan hair-removal clinic: her uniform so white it was almost blue, the potted plant in the corner of the room, the melancholy sound of a music box churning out synthesized versions of popular songs. Then it occurred to me that the towel laid out beneath my head was cruelly crushing the perm I'd had done at the hairdresser's just three days ago. Lifting my head slightly, I slipped a hand underneath to check the extent of the damage. The flattened spread of warm, limp hair felt as frail as a baby's.

The department store by the station was still open when I came out of the clinic, so I went in and browsed the new range of colors in the cosmetics section, splurged on a selection of Dean & DeLuca deli items for my dinner along with a baguette from the artisan bakery, then got on the train, half-intoxicated by this version of myself. From my earphones came the sweet voice of a Western singer. I couldn't understand the lyrics at all, but I assumed she must have been singing a love song. On the album cover that popped up on my screen, the singer's long tresses glistened like those of a fairy princess. Why hadn't I been born blond? I wondered to myself. Examining my reflection in the window of the train, I reached a hand up to touch my jet-black hair. In my next life, I decided, I would be blond. Then I would meet a gorgeous man with blond hair to match mine, and we would fall in love, and talk in English. In that incarnation, I would be surrounded with beautiful things, all day, every day. My life would be full of the sorts of things that brought instant contentment, and my heart would sing just to look at them. I would own so many wonderful things, I wouldn't know what to do with them, and then I would truly be happy.

I walked down the street with a spring in my step, practically skipping. On my way I passed the supermarket that by now would have started to reduce its prices before closing; next to it, the shop run by a wrinkly old couple selling Japanese sweets, its shutters already half down; then a mess of ripped posters for some yard sale that was happening or had already happened; and the barber's where I had never seen a single customer, only the owner who sat reading his newspaper by the window. Those things had no part to play in my world.

Back home in my one-bedroom apartment on the first floor of a three-story block, I'd just managed to arrange the selection of deli foods on my Scandinavian dining table, and press PLAY on the romantic comedy I'd chosen starring Michelle Williams, when the doorbell rang.

Life is full of dangers for a woman living by herself. I crept to the door silently so I could pretend I wasn't home if necessary. I peered through the peephole, but could see nobody.

The doorbell rang again. Who could it be? A pushy door-to-door salesman, somebody soliciting for some organization, a burglar, a rapist, a pair of rapists, a whole gang of armed rapists . . . and then another possibility occurred to me, appending itself to the terrifying list of options, and I found myself opening the door without having meant to. My aunt was standing outside.

"Auntie! What are you doing here?"

"Goodness gracious, what's happened to you? You look dreadful."

Examining my face with narrowed eyes, my aunt kicked off her cheap outlet-shop sandals so that they landed right on top of my Fabio Rusconi heels and Repetto ballerina pumps neatly arranged in the entrance.

"What a poky little doorway you've got!" she squawked before clumping through into my apartment.

"Your posture's a disgrace, too . . . But that's nothing new, I suppose. Come on, come on, stand up straight, that's it."

She tapped my spine with the back of her hand and I straightened up, staring in disbelief at the ugly scratches on the heels of the shoes she'd deposited in my doorway.

"Your hall's tiny too!" she exclaimed. "You're just like your mother! She had awful posture ever since she could walk. Born miserable, that one was. I was always pulling back her shoulders for her, but as soon as I let go she'd be straight back to slumping again. A person's character expresses itself in their body, you know. Oh heavens, look at all this!"

Without a moment's hesitation, my aunt sat down at my perfectly laid dinner table. The elegant minimalist chair, which matched the table, groaned as it accommodated a body significantly heavier than that of its usual sitter. I remained standing, staring incredulously at the finger-sized puncture that had appeared in the roast vegetable terrine. The film kept playing. The hair on Michelle Williams's arms shone beautifully in the sunlight, and I felt a wave of jealousy toward all the blond women in the world who had never had to give depilation a thought.

"Heavens, it was hot out there," my aunt said, flapping her collar to let in the air. "I've worked up a hell of a thirst. You don't have anything to drink, do you?" Through my aunt's synthetic sheer sweater with its cheap purple and gold sequins sewn into the shape of a tiger, I could see her graying undershirt. Her eyes followed me as I went to open the refrigerator.

"Goodness, even your fridge is tiny! I don't know how you can fit anything in there," she sniggered.

"I've only got perry," I said.

"Perry? What's that, then? Is it like sherry? Haven't you got any wine?"

My aunt took the drink I held out to her.

"What a measly little bottle! This won't go very far," she said as she took a big sip. Then she opened her mouth wide and smiled in satisfaction. "Ooh, it isn't bad, is it?"

My aunt stayed with me for dinner and watched the film through to the end. She didn't show much interest in the story line, her eyes roaming inquisitively around the room, but during the scene where Michelle Williams's character and another woman showered in the nude, her mouth fell open.

"You know, that's something I've always thought was strange! The hair on foreign women's arms and legs is so pale you can barely see it, but their hair down there is as dark as ours."

"Right," I agreed. She did have a point.

"I once heard that the color of people's hair down there is the same as the color of their eyebrows, but that can't be true, can it? I suppose that's the place that needs the most protection, so the body puts all its power into making the hair there as strong and dark as it can."

"Yeah, who knows."

"Come on, there's no use getting all embarrassed! I want to hear your real opinions about hair!"

Ignoring my aunt and the open palm she was striking on the table, I shoveled some Caesar salad into my mouth.

When the credits began rolling and I stopped the DVD, my aunt rested an arm on the table and leaned in conspiratorially toward me, as if she had been waiting all night for this moment.

"I think it's about time we got down to business," she said. "Tell me, young lady. What were you doing today?"

"Huh?" I stared in confusion at my aunt's face, which was etched with deep lines.

"Don't pretend you don't understand me. What do you think you're up to, eh? I know you've been deliberately weakening the power of your hair."

"The power of my hair?"

"I was so concerned, I came rushing straight over. And what do I find? Everything's all swish and swanky. It's horrible. And what's with all this pink rubbish you've got strewn around the place?"

My aunt held up between her thumb and forefinger the pink cushion she'd been leaning on, as if handling something unspeakably repulsive.

"Pink maximizes your romantic potential!" I cried. My aunt had succeeded in striking a nerve. I clenched my fists tight to hide my fuchsia-painted nails.

"What's the point of talking about 'romantic potential' when you go around with a face like you're sucking on a lemon?" my aunt said.

We glared at each other.

"Are you trying to pretend you're happy with your life? Is that it? You think I don't know all about that boyfriend who dumped you? Or that you only opened the door back there because you thought it might be him outside? Well, guess what? You landed me instead! Your old aunt sees ev-e-ry-thing, you know. Which is more than can be said for you! You didn't even notice he was two-timing you, all that time. What a sorry state of affairs! You must be totally and utterly stupid."

My aunt bulldozed on, tearing the lid off my Pandora's box like someone charging into a clearance sale, or ripping the wrapping paper off a present without a scrap of delicacy. My vision clouded, and I felt my blood drain right down to my toes.

"So, what's your plan, then? You've decided to start visiting these beauty salons, wasting your money on new clothes and makeup and all the rest so you can become beautiful and then have your revenge? Pah! You're far too easy to figure out. How utterly pathetic!" With this last jab, she shot me a grin. This was too much. I got to my feet to launch my counterattack. My aunt cocked her head, ready to take me on.

"You think it's okay just to barge into people's houses and say whatever the hell you want, do you?" I said. "I only held back when you first came in because I was trying not to hurt your feelings, but I don't see why I should bother! You certainly don't seem to care about hurting mine.

"I mean, you're dead, right? You died a year ago. Hanged yourself. Shigeru found you when he came home from the university. He was in terrible shock for a long time—still is, in fact. You shouldn't underestimate the kind of trauma you inflicted on him. And now you come around here, to see me? If you're going to appear as a ghost, if you *can* appear as a ghost, then it's Shigeru you should be visiting!"

Seeing that I'd run out of steam, my aunt scrunched up her nose, then waved her hands in a way that evoked total nonchalance.

"There's no need to worry about Shigeru. He's got his head screwed on straight, that one—even if he still insists on visiting my grave each month. If he's got that kind of energy, he'd be better off putting it into getting a girlfriend or two, I say. But he's a soppy fool, that kid. He always brings some food I used to like and leaves it there for me. It's enough to bring a tear to your eye. Come to think of it, could you do me a favor next time you see him and pass on a message from me? Tell him he doesn't need to come so often."

"How on earth am I supposed to say something like that to him?"

Feeling totally worn out all of a sudden, I fell back into my chair. Then I summoned up the courage to ask her something I'd never been able to ask her before.

"Why did you do it, Auntie?"

Of course, I thought as I formed the words, it stood

to reason that I hadn't been able to ask her—she'd been dead.

My aunt adopted a wheedling tone as she smiled. "Hey, you don't have anything sweet, do you?"

Reluctantly, I made some tea and brought out a packet of fine vanilla cookies I'd been saving for a special occasion. Only after she'd tasted them and found them to her liking did my aunt begin answering the question.

"I just got sick and tired of it all, really, of being what they used to call a 'kept woman.' This is Shigeru's father I'm talking about, of course, as I'm sure you know. We met when we were in our early twenties and fell in love, but he was already engaged, and so things just sort of went on like that, for thirty-odd years. Still, I was happy, all things considered. And then one day, out of the blue, he announced that he thought it was about time we ended it. He'd bought me my own place and my own bar, and of course he intended to keep supporting me for a while, but he'd decided that should be it between us. Can you believe that? And his tone of voice when he told me this, as though he was this generous, good man . . . I can't tell you how livid I was."

My aunt's memories seemed to grow clearer as she

talked, until it felt like she was describing something that had happened just yesterday. The fresher it all became, the angrier she got.

"So I did myself in. I didn't really think through what I was doing, and boy, did I regret it afterward. But at that time, I believed it would cause him the most damage. How wrong I was! I was stupid."

She stared into the distance. It was as if she was groping around in the depths of her memory, trying to isolate the precise moment where she had strayed off course—the part that she longed to do again, better.

Studying her face, I tried to remember what she'd looked like when she'd worked at the bar. It hadn't been a particularly classy place, and she hadn't worn a kimono, but she was always properly made up, always attentive to her clothes and her appearance. Even when she hadn't got it quite right, she was never without a thick coat of bright red lipstick, and she'd never given off the sad air of the discount store that she exuded now.

As I watched her, she turned to me, an expression of intense alertness on her face.

"Hey, you remember the time we went to watch the kabuki with your mom?"

The unexpected line of questioning startled me.

"I think you must have been still in grade school.

I'll never forget those gorgeous bento boxes we ate during the interval! But that's by the by. Remember the play we saw then? *The Maid of Dōjō Temple.*"

"The maid of what?"

"You know, the story where a woman is betrayed by the man that she loves, so she turns into a snake and climbs onto the temple where he lives and just dances and dances. You loved it at the time. Have you really forgotten? Pah! A heart of stone, you've got."

As my aunt jeered at me, I began scanning through the contents of my head, and soon enough a figure floated up in my imagination, accompanied by the beat of drums and the reedy strains of the bamboo flute. The figure was swaying, gliding, tilting, spinning around and around, never still for a second.

Back then, I hadn't been able to make out a word of what the kabuki actors said. Being just a child, I had trouble believing it was really Japanese they were speaking. In the first item of the program, middle-aged men came onto the stage one at a time, their faces painted white, talking at length in a language I couldn't understand. Some would go offstage when they were done, while others would stay on. I was bored silly, my bottom ached, and when the play finally finished, I felt nothing but relief.

During the interval, as my mother and aunt rolled the rubber bands off their bento boxes, they discussed how good or how sexy this or that actor or scene had been. I tried to explain how it felt not to comprehend any of the dialogue, but neither of them took me seriously. "What are you talking about?" they said. "They're speaking your language! Just listen carefully and you'll be fine!" As the curtains went up for the next item in the program, I comforted myself that if things got really bad, I could always slip out midway and take refuge in the foyer. At the back of the stage, I saw a group of men playing shamisen and drums and singing things I didn't understand, and just as my heart began to sink, a woman in a kimono—though really it was a man in a kimono, dressed as a woman— slipped out onto the stage and began to dance. That was Kiyohime.

Kiyohime was extraordinary. At first, her dance was a delicate, ladylike affair, but gradually her movements grew more and more powerful. There was something weird, almost otherworldly about that dance, and she went on dancing nonstop, like a mad thing, for about an hour. Kiyohime wore several kimonos on top of one another, which her assistants whipped off with perfect timing, so that, as she danced, she twirled from one beautiful kimono to the next, and the objects she held in her hands were magically transformed. It was like nothing I'd ever seen before, and I leaned forward in my seat to watch her precise movements as closely as I could. In the final scene of the play, Kiyohime used her power to possess the enormous temple bell, and as she stood brave and magnificent on top of it, her silver kimono sparkled.

After the play had ended, I was in a daze. I found my aunt peering at me with curiosity. "Here," she had said, pressing a dorayaki into my small palm. "Did you see that silver kimono Kiyohime wore at the end? The glittery one?"

I nodded.

"Snake scales," she'd said as she nodded back.

"Kiyohime was wonderful, wasn't she?" my aunt said now. "So persistent, so dynamic."

She rested her chin on her hands theatrically, and continued, all dreamy-eyed, "I should've done the same thing, you know. I should've stuck in there, like she did, become a snake, done whatever it took. Thirty years we were together! I don't know what I was thinking, trying to act cool and composed when

I'd just been dumped. Playing the grown-up, then going home and hanging myself. I mean, really! It was pathetic. I'd have been far better off placing a deadly curse on him. I'd have had every right, too. It was what he deserved. For all his show of so-called chivalry, he just did whatever the hell he wanted. There's nothing less sexy than that."

With that, my aunt took a big bite of a cookie and munched noisily. "So that's why I'm developing a special trick."

"A special trick?"

"I reckon it's still not too late. I've spent this past year learning how to appear like this."

"Wait, this is a skill you learned?"

"You bet! All the fruit of my own labors."

"Well, it's quite a trick!"

"Don't be silly! This is nothing. There's no punch to it. I know you thought the same, when I first turned up at the door. You wondered why, if I was a ghost, I was showing up at the door like a regular visitor. I want a special skill that's truly awesome. Something terrifying enough to scar him for life."

"Huh." Not knowing what I was supposed to say, I stuffed a cookie into my mouth. It was delicious, but I felt that the taste was a bit too delicate in some way, the perfume of vanilla too faint. I wondered now if I'd actually eaten the dorayaki that my aunt had given me in the theater all those years ago, its sponge patties oozing with sweet bean jam.

"Anyway, I'm sure you understand what I'm getting at, don't you? You can't let the power of your hair slip away from you. You think you have to spruce yourself up after being dumped by that two-timing idiot—that's why you started going to that hair-removal place. Can't you see that it's pointless? Your hair is the only wild thing you have left—the one precious crop of wildness remaining to you. I want you to think long and hard about what you could do with it. Rather than getting all sore because you got dumped by some worthless scumbag, I want you to fight, like Kiyohime did. Your hair is your power!"

I hadn't failed to register how grating and how batty each and every one of my aunt's statements was, and as I reflected, I recalled that she'd had these kinds of tendencies before she'd died, too. In fact, I began remembering all sorts of things about her—how out of nowhere she'd started going on about "the force of nature," producing huge batches of handmade soap and hennaing her hair a dirty reddish shade. She'd been an interesting person, I thought. Why did she have to die? Now, for the first time, I felt like I understood where she was coming from. I even felt grateful toward her for choosing to visit me over Shigeru, despite the black cloud that had, quite understandably, been hanging over him since her death.

"But Kiyohime turns into a snake, right? Snakes don't have any hair at all," I joked.

"That's not what I'm saying." My aunt seemed totally bored by my pedantry. "Did you know that in some performances of *The Maid of Dōjō Temple*, they have two dancing maids?" She shot me a great sassy smile, as if she were once again wearing the bright red lipstick of bygone days. Then, her expression suddenly serious, she took my slender hands in hers, pink nails and all.

"Let's become monsters together," she said, looking straight into my eyes.

"When my special trick is ready, I'll make sure you're the first to see it before I try it out for real."

Those had been my aunt's parting words as she left—through the door. *But you're a ghost* was the thought that had run through my head.

I tried speaking it out loud now in the bathhouse. "But you're a ghost!"

The damp, dense steam pervading the bathing area masked my softly spoken words.

Yet my aunt had been nothing like I imagined ghosts to be. Compared to me—a comatose coward who had spent two months cramming her head with all kinds of strange affirmations so as to pretend she was doing fine when really she was anything but—my aunt was spilling over with life.

Vigorously lathering my skin with my organic soap, I remembered my aunt's words. She wanted me to "think long and hard" about what I could do with my hair. What on earth did that mean? It was just hair, for goodness' sake.

But when I thought it through more deeply, I realized I didn't think about it as "just hair," after all. Hair was a problem that I carried around with me constantly. However much I shaved or plucked, it would always grow back again. It was like some everlasting exercise regime. And it wasn't just me, either—all women were prisoners of their body hair. An image of all those women in the waiting room of the laser treatment clinic came floating back to me. It was the same here, in the public bathhouse. The ladies' bath was heaving with women of all ages, many of them sliding razors over their arms or legs as they washed themselves. Bits of black hair swathed in foam went sailing down the drains.

I suppose I should explain at this point that my bathroom boiler mysteriously stopped working the night of my aunt's visit, which was why I found myself in a public bathhouse. Perhaps it was the shock of her appearance that did it. I found the whole occurrence difficult to wrap my head around—a broken boiler, in the twenty-first century! In fact, the idea of having a twenty-first-century bath that relied on an old-fashioned balanced-flue boiler for its hot water was pretty insane as it was. That night, after my aunt had left, I'd stood there stark naked, flicking the lever over and over to try to get it to start, but the only response I got was a sad, muffled click that echoed across the bathroom walls. When I finally gave up and called the manufacturers, they informed me coolly that the earliest repair appointment they could give me would be in two days' time. Two days' time! The twenty-first century certainly wasn't like this in the films I'd watched or the manga I'd read when I was younger. A twenty-first century where balanced-flue boilers and public baths still existed seemed like some kind of a con.

As it was, there I sat in the bathhouse that same

evening, surrounded by women passing razors over their bodies, leaving their skin smooth and hair-free. It seemed to me unquestionable that it looked better. But *when* had it become better? Who had first been struck by the notion that skin would be more attractive if it was shaved? Who had been the first woman to shave? How had other people around them been convinced by their logic and begun shaving themselves? Why had I, born such a long time after them, come to think the same? Why, in the twenty-first century, did I have to fork out huge sums of money to go to the hair-removal clinic? Removing hair was the sort of thing you would think could be done painlessly, in an instant, what with all our amazing twenty-first-century technology.

Whenever the plastic washbasins and chairs scraped along the floor, they produced comic squeals that echoed through the big room. Around me I could see women with smooth, hairless skin; women who had not shaved in a while; and old women who didn't seem to care about the little hair that was still left on their bodies. Why was hair such an inescapable concern for us? Suddenly fearing that all this scrutinizing of other people's hair was going to turn me into some kind of pervert, I picked up the shower handle and began energetically massaging shampoo into my head of wet hair to divert my own attention.

On that hateful day that he dumped me, I had forgotten to shave. As soon as I'd realized, I'd begun worrying about whether he'd notice, debating whether or not I'd get away with it, cursing the fact that I'd worn short sleeves, obsessing over the few odd hairs scattered across my arms, trying to remember how long the hairs on my knuckles were and casually checking to see—and that was what I'd been doing when he mumbled something from across the table, something I couldn't hear because he was speaking so quietly and because my mind had been wholly occupied with thoughts of my hair. I just said, "What?" and then the next thing I knew he was apologizing to me.

On the train back home later that day, I found my eyes rooted to one of the myriad advertisements for hair-removal clinics in front of me, although I'd never before even given them so much as a passing glance. The ad showed a picture of a beautiful woman with a broad smile on her face, and smooth legs extending from beneath her shorts. Long, pale, iridescent legs—now that I think about it, they were just like white snakes. The more I stared at that advert, the more it became obvious: the horrible thing that had just happened had happened because I wasn't depilated. It had happened because my arms, my legs, and other parts of my body were not perfectly hairless—because I was an unkempt person who went about life as if there was nothing wrong with being hairy. That was why I had been dumped and cheated on, because the whole time, it turned out, he had been comparing the state of my hairy body with another woman's, and had chosen between us accordingly. Those kinds of thoughts had flooded into my head with tremendous momentum, one after the other, and before I knew it, my desire to be free of the problem of hair seemed overpowering. I didn't want to have to think about it anymore. In that moment, as all my strength drained out of me, I dreamed only of total hairlessness.

Rinsing the shampoo out of my hair now, I wondered why my aunt had come along and denied me that kind of freedom. I was sick of hair, utterly sick. Going around thinking about it constantly was a damn hassle. If I smartened myself up, made my skin hairless and smooth, then I was sure to meet a wonderful new man. Why did my aunt have to come and pour cold water all over my lovely, optimistic thoughts?

As I waited for the conditioner to sink in, I inspected my arms one at a time, both hair-free as a result of that day's treatment. *You see, Auntie? See how good they look?* As I stroked each arm in turn, I felt the tears run down my cheeks. I hurriedly turned the shower on my face to conceal them.

The thing was, my aunt was absolutely right, and I knew it. Being hairless didn't get you anywhere. It didn't change a single thing. What an idiot I'd been! All those stupid, selfish things he'd come out with, like how his feelings for the other woman had "grown." Had he been gauging his feelings with a measuring tape or something? And what did I go and say in response? "Well, I guess these things happen." What a weed! At the very least I should have gotten angry. If I'd just thought about it, I'd have seen that everything he was saying was a load of shit, but instead I just bore it as best I could. And why? Why? Had I been brainwashed or what?

One after another, the little boxes where my memories had been stored had their lids flipped open, and the memories came together to form a black, hazy mass.

I'm coming, the black mass told me, as it swelled larger and larger. I opened more boxes. I kept on opening them, but there were always more. Still more. I groped around blindly, feeling every last one. *I'm coming, I'm coming, I'm on my way,* the black mass kept telling me. Not many left to go now; I had nearly unearthed them all. I could hear the blackness clamoring, the blackness I knew to be the accumulation of all the sadness and rage and frustration and emptiness and idiocy I'd been storing up inside my body. Just three left to go, no, four, now three, two, and this, this is the last box right here. *I'm coming,* announced the mass, right underneath my skin, so close that its voice struck me right between the shoulders. *I'm coming,* and then the black force overtook me, propelling itself out of my body.

Feeling a strange sensation beneath my palms, I opened my eyes and looked down. My thighs were black. Through the steam on the surface of the mirror opposite me, I could make out something that looked like a black demon. I touched my face. It felt no different from the hair on my head. My limbs, my torso, every single part of my body was covered with hair, from head to toe. Glossy, pitch-black hair, not a single split end or damaged strand. There was no trace left of my perm, either.

Before I knew it, I was standing with my arms stretched out in front of me, staring at myself in rapture. To know that all along my body had contained hair this strong, this black, this magnificent was an amazing thing—I was an amazing thing!

Glancing around, I discovered that the women in the bathhouse were staring at me with a mixture of alarm and curiosity. And with good reason: it must have seemed to them like a hairy monster of unknown origin had materialized out of nowhere.

Uh-oh, I thought. I stood up quickly and ran to the door. The stool I'd been sitting on clattered onto its side behind me. In the changing room, as the women around me screamed and whimpered, I retrieved my bag from my locker as casually as I could. I left the bathhouse quietly and turned down a deserted shopping street, running as fast as my legs would carry me. My steady pace and the night breeze worked together like a hair dryer, draining the moisture from the hair that covered my body. It felt good. Really good.

When I got back home, I stood in front of my full-length mirror, staring at the mystery creature in front of me: neither bear nor ape, but some other being entirely, covered head to toe in glossy, slightly damp hair. The hair looked a bit like that of Sadako from *The Ring*, although it was only about half the length of hers. Actually, when I thought about it, I came to the realization that Sadako was a pretty impressive character. Not only could she emerge from wells, she could also come out of the TV set. Now, that was a special trick! And the same went for Okiku, Oiwa, and all the other famous ghosts I could think of. They all deserved credit. The ability to appear as a ghost was proof of an iron will.

Something terrible startled me out of my reverie. On both my arms, just where I'd had the permanent hair removal done, was a patch of hair much thinner than the rest and clearly much weaker. In terms of strength, shine, body—it was inferior in every way. What had I gone and done? Another anxious thought followed. Transforming into a monster was all very well, but what on earth was I supposed to do now?

My program of hair fortification began the following morning.

I have started eating as much liver and seaweed as I can. Beans and eggs are supposed to be good, too. As I massage horse oil over the damaged patches on my arms, I repeatedly apologize to the follicles. Naturally, I apply the oil to other parts of my body, too.

Now that I've developed an understanding with the black mass inside me, I can retract it at will, so it doesn't interfere with my work. Just like my colleagues who spend their free time taking courses or pursuing various leisure activities, I pour my energy into fostering the power of my hair.

Every day before bed, I transform in order to assess how my hair is coming along. Then I brush it thoroughly, using a luxury boar-bristle brush. I don't know how much of it is the work of the horse oil, but the weak patches on my arms are now almost indistinguishable from the rest of me, so I've started pondering what my next move should be. I haven't reached any conclusions.

I'm going to keep mulling it over until I land on a way to put my hair to good use—until I can devise my own unique trick. In the meantime, I intend to keep taking good care of it. That way, when the opportunity arises for me to unleash my power in a dramatic fashion like Kiyohime, I'll be able to rise to the occasion. Kiyohime was free of hair and I am full of it, but I think our ambitions are the same. I want a skill, a special power into which I can throw my whole self. As to the question of what kind of creature I am, I really couldn't care less. It doesn't bother me if I stay a nameless monster.

My aunt hasn't shown up to see me yet, so I guess

she hasn't managed to perfect her special trick. I'm sure that whatever she comes up with will be unspeakably brilliant. I really hope she comes back soon. Until then, I'll keep working on myself, always holding at the forefront of my mind the image of my aunt and myself, dancing together, kimonos twinkling.

The Peony Lanterns

"Good evening to you, sir!"

He'd ignored the doorbell three times already when he heard the woman's voice carrying through the thick steel door. Sitting on his sofa, Shinzaburō froze in alarm, hardly breathing. His body felt terribly heavy, and the thought of getting up was unbearable. Usually in this situation, Shinzaburō would have relied on his wife to answer the door, but with it being Obon, she was away visiting her parents. Besides, it was ten o'clock at night. Shinzaburō had no idea who his visitor was, but he believed that ringing people's doorbells at this hour was unreasonable behavior—and

Shinzaburō disliked people who behaved unreasonably. From a young age, he had been instilled with a firm grasp on what was and wasn't reasonable. In his adult life, throughout his career as a salesperson, his professional conduct had always been eminently reasonable. Even when he'd been laid off as part of the company's post-recession restructure, he had retained his sense of reason and walked away without a fuss.

That had been more than six months ago. Shinzaburō's wife had begun dropping gentle hints that he should find himself another job. He knew she was right—but somehow he couldn't bring himself to do it. Both his mind and body felt leaden. Whenever he browsed job listings online he was hit by the unshakable sense that he was being made a fool of, and he couldn't stand the idea of visiting the employment bureau either. Had he really become the sort of man who had to rely on an employment bureau? The very idea seemed too wretched to bear. And there he'd been believing that he was talented and had something to offer the world. He'd gone about his life not being a nuisance to anyone, playing by the rules, acting reasonably at all times. How had it come to this?

While his wife was at work, Shinzaburō would do a bit of housework, but a token offering was as far as it went. The truth of the matter was this: spending all his time in his marl-gray tracksuit, shabby from constant wear, Shinzaburō had morphed into a big gray sloth. In the afternoon, he would lounge about on the sofa, watching reruns of period dramas and mulling over questions of no particular significance, like whether, back in the Edo period, his lack of fixed employment would have made him a rōnin. How much better that sounded than simply *unemployed.*

"Good evening to you, sir!"

The same voice again. From the light filtering through the living room curtain, it must have been obvious to whoever was outside that there was someone at home.

"Oh, damn it all!"

Shinzaburō got up from the sofa, slowly crept toward the door to avoid his presence being discovered—though he knew from long years of experience that such a thing was impossible—and peered through the peephole.

Outside the gate stood two women. They were dressed in practically identical outfits: black suits, white shirts, sheer tights, and black pumps. One was somewhere between forty and fifty, and the other looked to be in her early thirties. The elder was staring with terrifying intensity at the peephole, while the younger was shyly inspecting her feet. They made for an altogether peculiar pair. Immediately, alarm bells went off in Shinzaburō's head. No one in his right mind would involve himself in a situation he knew would be troublesome from the outset. In this particular period of his life, Shinzaburō did not have the mental energy to spare on that kind of nonsense.

The women seemed to sense Shinzaburō's presence in his cramped entranceway, and the elder one piped up again. "Good evening to you, sir!"

Shinzaburō guessed she must be the one who had done all the speaking so far. The younger one kept her head down, not moving a muscle. Something about the way she held one cheek angled toward the door suggested she was invested in what the person on the other side thought of her. Indeed, the way she carried herself was common among highly self-conscious women, thought Shinzaburō. The observational skills he had cultivated during his years as a sales representative, which enabled him to pick up on these little details about people, were a source of great pride to him.

Very cautiously, Shinzaburō opened his mouth. "Yes, what is it?"

"Oh, good evening, sir," began the elder woman

with an affected smile on her face. "We are door-to-door sales representatives, visiting the homes in this area in the best of faith. We are terribly sorry to disturb you at this hour, but we were wondering if you might be able to spare us a couple of minutes of your time."

Something about the woman's voice filled Shinzaburō with instantaneous exhaustion. He felt nothing but loathing for these stupid women who'd invaded his precious relaxation time and forced him to walk all the way to the front door. *Don't you know that I'm exhausted?* he wanted to say. *For six whole months now, I've been totally and utterly exhausted.*

"No, thanks, I'm afraid not. It's late."

No sooner had Shinzaburō delivered his curt answer, which he had hoped would make them go away, than the younger one, who had been examining the floor so intently, raised her head to look toward the peephole, and said in a weak, sinuous voice, "Come now, don't be so inhospitable! *Open up!*"

If a willow tree could speak, Shinzaburō thought, this is the kind of voice it would have. He blinked and found himself in the living room, the two women facing him across the coffee table. As if that wasn't bad enough, they were sitting on the sofa, while Shinzaburō had been relegated to one of the more uncomfortable kitchen chairs he and his wife had bought online. He had no memory of carrying it into this room. Sandwiched beneath his buttocks was one of the Marimekko cushions his wife loved so much. Shinzaburō still had no idea what its pattern was supposed to represent, although right now that was hardly his most pressing concern.

While Shinzaburō was still wondering how on earth he had wound up here, the women sat looking at him, their four stockinged kneecaps arranged into a perfect row of iridescent silver. Seeing that they had his attention, they both pulled the same inscrutable expression and handed him business cards as white as their papery faces.

"Allow us to introduce ourselves."

Flummoxed by being handed two cards at exactly the same time, Shinzaburō somehow managed to accept both and examined the names printed on them. The elder woman was Yoneko Mochizuki, the younger Tsuyuko Iijima.

Just then, Shinzaburō's eyes fell on three steaming cups of green tea placed on the coffee table. Did I go and make tea without realizing it? he thought. Surely these two didn't sneak into the kitchen and make it themselves? What's more, he noticed that the yōkan he'd been saving for a special occasion was there too, cut into neat slices. As Shinzaburō was trying to wrap his head around all this, Yoneko spoke.

"We took the liberty of examining the nameplate outside your door. It's Mr. Hagiwara, is that right? Oh, good. Forgive our impertinence, but may we ask your first name?"

Why did they need to know? "It's Shinzaburō," he found himself saying, though he'd had no inclination to answer the question. It was as if his mouth was moving of its own accord.

"Shin-za-bu-rō," Tsuyuko pronounced slowly.

Having his first name spoken like that by someone he'd only just met made him shudder. It was much too intimate.

"It's an absolute pleasure to make your acquaintance, Shinzaburō."

Between this woman's honeyed tone and her flirtatious manner, there was definitely something overfamiliar about her. Shinzaburō averted his eyes. Did she think her looks would allow her to get away with such behavior? Sure, with her alabaster skin, her hair lustrous as a raven's coat, and all those coquettish sideways glances, she was undoubtedly beautiful. And yet, despite all these gifts, the epithet that seemed to fit Tsuyuko like no other was *misfortunate*.

Without waiting for an invitation, Tsuyuko took a sip of tea from her cup, leaving a sticky red lipstick mark on its rim. It came to Shinzaburō in a flash that as far as sales work was concerned, this woman was probably utterly incompetent. The same went for her companion, too.

"Well, if you don't mind, we'll get down to business," said Yoneko, projecting her gray-haired head forward like a tortoise emerging from its shell. Shinzaburō nodded reluctantly, resolving to hear out their patter and then get them to leave. Changing the key of her already gloomy expression so it was positively funereal, Yoneko began to speak.

"Miss Tsuyuko here has had the *most* lamentable of lives, Mr. Hagiwara. She was born into a family of great repute and prestige, and yet here she is now, as you see, working all day long as a mere saleswoman. The cause of this tragic downfall was that her beloved mother passed away at a young age, leaving poor little Tsuyuko behind. Her father was a kind man, but rather weak of character, and it wasn't long before he developed an intimate relationship with the maidservant. As sad as it is to admit, it would appear that there are a great many weak-willed men out there. As for the maidservant, well! I know that of late people take leaks of personal information and so forth awfully seriously, but we do *so* much wish you to hear this story in its entirety, so I will on this occasion divulge that her name is Kuniko. Now, Mr. Hagiwara, we do most earnestly beseech you to exercise the utmost caution around women going by the name of Kuniko. For the thing is, you see, this Kuniko utilized her feminine wiles to claw her way to the stature of second wife. As if that wasn't enough, she then resolved to gain sole possession of Tsuyuko's father's fortune, and began spoon-feeding him all kinds of groundless fabrications about Tsuyuko, morning and night . . . he was not a man of strong character. Honestly, men like that really are the worst, aren't they, Mr. Hagiwara? Anyhow, predictably enough, he foolishly believed every word that Kuniko spouted, and began to look coldly upon his daughter. Unable to bear this cruel treatment, Tsuyuko left home without even finishing high school. Her life from that point on has been one tear-inducing episode after another. To start—"

"Sorry, but why are you telling me all this?" Shinzaburō finally broke in on her lament. For a long time, he had been stunned into silence by Yoneko's phenomenal pace of speaking, which would have rivaled that of any rakugo performer, but eventually he managed to find his opening. "What does any of this have to do with me?"

At this obviously unexpected interruption, a look of unbridled annoyance flashed across Yoneko's face, but she continued with a cool expression. "It has nothing to do with you *personally*, Mr. Hagiwara, but the fact that we have met in this way implies some kind of indelible connection between us. It's Miss Tsuyuko's heartfelt wish that you hear her story."

Tsuyuko nodded in agreement, dabbing her tears with a white handkerchief that had miraculously appeared in her hand.

"You came barging in here! Does that qualify as an 'indelible connection'? Besides, you're acting very oddly, if you don't mind me saying so! First, you said you were here as sales representatives, and now you're here telling me your life story! Don't you think that's a bit inappropriate?"

As Shinzaburō began to lay down the laws of reason to these two utterly unreasonable women, they met him with expressions of genuine incomprehension.

"What exactly is wrong with that?"

"Now look here," said Shinzaburō. "Don't feign ignorance with me. I used to be a salesman too, so I know the score. Forcing your way into people's houses and then acting like this is just not how it's done."

"Oh, Mr. Hagiwara! So you were in the sales industry too! Well, that only proves our indelible connection. Isn't that just wonderful, Tsuyuko?"

"Oh yes, Yoneko!"

Shinzaburō looked on in horror as the two beamed at each other.

"But Mr. Hagiwara, your use of the past tense suggests you've given the profession up. Forgive my impertinence, but why is that? Would it be anything to do with restructuring, which has become so common in the business world of late?" Yoneko cocked her head and stared pointedly at Shinzaburō. This person was utterly unsuited to sales, Shinzaburō thought. Most likely she hadn't even been through training. In his incredulity, he found himself answering her question without ever having meant to.

"Yes, that's right. I lost my job when my company was restructured."

As Shinzaburō spoke, he was all too aware that his head hung in embarrassment, as if of its own volition. He realized that this was the first time he'd spoken about what had happened to him to anybody other than his wife.

"Oh, Shinzaburō! What a terrible shame!" Tsuyuko said in a shrill voice, a hint of a smile perhaps meant to signify compassion hovering around her mouth. She leaned her slender body over the table toward him and rested her thin fingers gently on Shinzaburō's forearm. Startled by the coldness of her touch, Shinzaburō hurriedly crossed his arms so as to shrug off any contact. Tsuyuko shot him a look that seemed to say, *Well, fine, be like that.* She turned away coyly for a moment, then looked back at him, more brazen than ever. Once again, Shinzaburō averted his gaze.

"Oh, Tsuyuko! How kindhearted you are! And what frostiness you are shown in return! Mr. Hagiwara, why is it that you feel no sympathy for Miss Tsuyuko?"

"Of course I feel bad for her, but that's not the issue here! Besides, from what I've heard so far, it hardly sounds like the most unusual of tales. Every life has its dose of misfortune."

At Shinzaburō's words, the two widened their eyes in a charade of disbelief.

In a tone of utter astonishment Yoneko said, "My, what a horrendous age we are living in! In days of yore, anyone who beheld Tsuyuko's great beauty and heard even a snippet of her tragic tale would be overwhelmed by sympathy and agree to commit lovers' suicide with her on the spot! Isn't that right, Miss Tsuyuko?"

Tsuyuko pressed her handkerchief to her eyes again and nodded with even greater fervor than before, then dissolved into gasping, theatrical sobs. She had to be faking it, Shinzaburō thought. He was getting more and more irritated with the duo's outrageous behavior, and before he knew it, he was saying, "Okay then, what about you two? Are you not going to say anything about my layoff? That seems pretty heartless to me! If you think I should be feeling sympathy for you, then I expect the same in return."

Yet as Shinzaburō ended his frustrated outpouring, he saw that Tsuyuko and Yoneko wore expressions of total indifference. As he sat there unnerved by this transformation, Yoneko said with insouciance, "Well, men are the stronger sex. You are the blessed ones. Everything will turn out right for you in the end, I'm sure. I don't have the least concern about you. What worries me is Miss Tsuyuko. Women are so utterly powerless. Can Miss Tsuyuko really go through her life as a single woman? I ask myself. Can she endure this way? Hmm, what's that? The same goes for me, you're thinking? Oh, you really need not worry about me. Please concern yourself solely with Miss Tsuyuko. And just to be clear, I'm not ordering you to commit lovers' suicide. We have no wish to place that kind of burden on your shoulders. What we would like is for you to purchase our product."

Shinzaburō had not been conscious of any ongoing preparations, but now, with timing that seemed almost too impeccable, Tsuyuko set something down on the table with a thump.

It was some kind of lantern thing. Didn't those have some special name?

"It's a tōrō, Mr. Hagiwara," said Yoneko with a triumphant grin, as if she'd read his thoughts. These two were really too much to take.

"Of late, these portable lanterns are enjoying a surprising revival, Mr. Hagiwara! You'll find they're far more fashionable than flashlights! Many customers like to coordinate them with the design of their yukata when attending summer festivals, and now that it's Obon, they're great for hanging outside the house to welcome home the souls of the returning dead. Honestly, they are extremely popular! The exterior is silk crepe with a peony pattern and is very well received by the ladies. Do you happen to be married, Mr. Hagiwara? I believe you are, aren't you?"

"Oh, Shinzaburō!" exclaimed Tsuyuko in a high voice. "How absolutely despicable of you! What about me?"

"Oh, Miss Tsuyuko, how cruel destiny can be! I tell you, she really does have the most awful luck with men. I go out of my mind with worry. Now, where was I? Oh yes, I was just saying that these peony tōrō lanterns are extremely popular with the ladies. Your wife will be absolutely delighted, I am sure. I have heard that those from Western climes are good at surprising their lady friends with flowers and such little gestures of their affection, but males from Japan often neglect to do such things. Don't get me wrong—I'm not trying to suggest that the same is true of you, Mr. Hagiwara! Only that with your unemployment causing your wife such hardship, occasionally gifting things that women like, these lanterns for example, is a rather good strategy, by which I mean to say—it wouldn't do you any harm, would it?"

"Oh, Shinzaburō! How it grieves me to think of you giving presents to another woman!"

"There there, Miss Tsuyuko. Do calm yourself. I'm quite sure that Shinzaburō will be buying two lanterns, one of which he will of course be presenting to you!"

"Oh, Miss Yoneko, what are you saying! There is no way that a man as considerate as Shinzaburō would forget about you! He shall be buying three lanterns, for sure! Three, at the very least."

So this is their sales strategy, thought Shinzaburō, utterly aghast. After watching them prattle on at each other for a while, he felt he'd had enough of being neglected.

"Look, I'm sorry, but I don't want any of your lanterns. Contrary to what you seem to think, if I go around buying such stuff while I'm without an income, the only thanks I'll get from my wife will be a good telling-off."

There was a second's pause and then a sickly, snake-like voice came slithering out of Tsuyuko's mouth.

"Then we shall resent you, Shinzaburō."

"W-what?"

"We will resent you," she repeated, fixing him with a withering look.

"Now, now, Tsuyuko," said Yoneko. "It will not do to rush Mr. Hagiwara into a decision. We mustn't pressure him. Let's allow him first to experience our much-vaunted lanterns. I have no doubt he'll be delighted by them. Mr. Hagiwara, would you mind advising me where your light switch is?"

Shinzaburō looked toward the switch and, as if in silent understanding, the lights in the room immediately dimmed. Before Shinzaburō had time to register his surprise, the lantern on the table swelled with light, illuminating the darkened room.

On the other side floated the green-white faces of the two women. Shinzaburō remembered playing this kind of game with his friends at school—everyone shining flashlights under their faces to try to scare one another. Finally acclimatizing to the evening's unrelenting stream of reason-defying events, Shinzaburō was sufficiently relaxed to reminiscence about his boyhood. Filtering through the peonies, the soft lantern light spilled into the room. It was as if another world had materialized, right there in his living room. With their legs concealed under the table, the women looked as if they consisted of their upper bodies alone, free-floating in the air.

"You two look just like gho—I mean, you seem somehow not of this world."

Immediately regretting his choice of words, Shinzaburō grimaced.

"You mean *us*?" asked Yoneko with a wry smile. She seemed not at all displeased by the remark.

"And what would you do if we were . . . *not of this world*?" asked Tsuyuko, looking up at him through her eyelashes, lips iridescent with gloss, or spit, or something else entirely. Then, without waiting for his answer, the two women dissolved into a fit of giggles.

The lights in the room blinked on.

"So you see, that's how it works. It's a rather good product, wouldn't you say?" Yoneko and Tsuyuko smiled in unison.

"Indeed, but I really don't need it," said Shinzaburō. The two women shared a glance and nodded gravely. When they turned to look at Shinzaburō again, their faces bore entirely different expressions.

"If you don't buy our lanterns, Shinzaburō, I will perish," said Tsuyuko.

"Now, Mr. Hagiwara, did you hear that? Miss Tsuyuko says she's going to perish," said Yoneko.

"Do what you like to me, I'm not going to leave here until Shinzaburō buys some!" said Tsuyuko, breaking into a screechy voice like a child throwing a tantrum.

"Oh, listen to that!" Yoneko went on persistently in a low murmur. "If your wife comes home and sees Tsuyuko here, she'll be terribly jealous, won't she,

Mr. Hagiwara? If only you would buy a lantern, we'd leave immediately." While Yoneko was speaking, she and Tsuyuko snuck glances at Shinzaburō.

"I said I wasn't going to buy one," said Shinzaburō firmly. The more excitable the two women grew, the more he found himself regaining his composure.

"Did you hear that, Miss Tsuyuko? You'd be better off giving up on a rotten-hearted man like this one."

"No, Miss Yoneko. I trust him. I trust dear Shinzaburō."

"Now, Mr. Hagiwara. Did you hear what Miss Tsuyuko just said? How awfully touching."

Observing the farce being played out before his eyes, Shinzaburō found himself unexpectedly marveling at their teamwork. Yoneko was stunning in her supporting role. There was no way Tsuyuko alone would have garnered such impact. Their methods certainly ran against the grain of traditional sales techniques, but it had to be said there was something formidable about them. It must be down to desperation, Shinzaburō thought—desperation at their lack of success. He even began to consider just buying one of the damned things out of pity, but when he pictured his wife's expression upon seeing the new acquisition, the temptation fizzled away. For two or three years now, his wife had only had eyes for Scandinavian homeware, not this traditional Japanese decor.

Tsuyuko and Yoneko were keeping up their noisy masquerade. With sudden clarity he saw that whether he chose to buy a lantern or not, hell awaited him regardless.

The next thing he knew, Shinzaburō was laughing out loud. It felt like a long time since he'd laughed properly like this. If push came to shove, he thought as he chuckled, you could carry on life like these goofballs did, and you'd still be fine. Well, depending on your definition of *fine*, of course—but at any rate, nothing terrible would happen to you if you broke the rules. With that thought, Shinzaburō felt a hot surge behind his eyes, and quickly clenched his teeth.

Apparently unnerved by this alteration in him, Yoneko and Tsuyuko spoke.

"Have you had a change of heart, Mr. Hagiwara?"

"Have you decided to accommodate my request, Shinzaburō?"

"No, I'm not going to buy a lantern. But still, thank you, nonetheless." His voice sounded dignified, somehow, and free. When he next looked, Tsuyuko and Yoneko appeared to be suspended in midair. The next moment, the lights in the room went off again, as if someone had blown out all the candles.

Shinzaburō woke to the sound of sparrows cheeping outside the window. He lifted his head from the living room floor and saw four lanterns strewn about him. Tsuyuko and Yoneko were nowhere to be seen.

At the sound of keys in the door, Shinzaburō quickly sat up and prepared himself for the next onslaught. But the person who came rushing into the room with a loud "Hi! I'm home!" carrying her suitcase so the wheels didn't leave marks on the floor, was his wife. Taking in the messy room, with Shinzaburō stretched out sloppily on the floor, she frowned and said in a tone of utter disbelief, "Oh, for heaven's sake!"

Shinzaburō couldn't help but notice that her gestures and her expressions weren't unlike those of Tsuyuko and Yoneko. Why did all women pull the same face when they looked at him?

"What have you been doing in here? I thought you were supposed to be looking for a job while I was gone! And what on earth are these? Some kind of failed DIY experiment?"

Listening to his wife's protestations as she picked

up the lanterns littering the room, Shinzaburō thought of his wallet, which would probably be a few notes lighter, and a pang of dread spread through him. Of course, for a salesperson to take money without permission went against every rule in the book, but he wouldn't have put it past those two. It was basically theft! How much were they charging for those blasted lanterns, anyway? Ah, there was nothing for it—now he really would have to find a job as soon as possible. Shinzaburō gingerly pulled himself up from the floor, where a pool of light filtering through the curtain gently flickered.

Shinzaburō spotted Tsuyuko and Yoneko only once after that encounter.

He'd been on the early shift at his new workplace and was back home preparing dinner when he heard a woman's voice outside the window. Peering through a gap in the curtain, he saw the two of them standing at the gate next to the nameplate. They appeared to be in serious conversation.

Shinzaburō remembered. It had slipped his mind entirely, but after coaxing the truth about the peony lanterns out of Shinzaburō, his wife had bought a sticker at the home goods store that read NO SALES VISITORS! and had stuck it up next to their nameplate. That had been about a year ago now. The business cards they had given him that evening many months ago had mysteriously vanished, and for some reason he couldn't recall the name of their company, though he was sure he'd made a mental note of it.

"There's one here, too! How cruel."

"We can't go in now, not with this talisman stuck up . . . What a pity!"

"It's so heartless."

"It really is sheer heartlessness."

Tsuyuko and Yoneko were wearing the same outfits as before.

A talisman, indeed! Shinzaburō smirked. Such melodrama, as usual! Just what exactly was the deal with these two? And yet he couldn't deny that he was a little bit pleased to have seen them again. The next moment, they both looked toward the window in unison and Shinzaburō lunged away from the curtain.

My Superpower

Questions with Kumiko
No. 9: So, what's your superpower?

I'll begin by pointing out what Okon and Oiwa have in common: both their faces swelled up something terrible. As you are doubtless aware, both women became disfigured—one from being poisoned, the other through disease. Both subsequently became ghosts, avenging those who had brought about their ruin.

Since childhood, I've observed the way both Okon and Oiwa are portrayed on TV and in films as terrifying monsters. That's the form people expect them to take. Ultimately, that's just the way that the horror genre works, whatever world you're living in. It's no fun if zombies don't rise up from the dead, if Carrie isn't drenched in pig's blood. Walls need to be splashed and plates need to be smashed. Without all that violence and gore, viewers simply switch off.

But the thing is, I never thought of Okon and Oiwa as terrifying monsters. If they were terrifying, so was I. If they were monsters, that meant I was a monster too. I knew that much instinctively.

I'm of an allergic disposition. I have extremely sensitive skin, and I've suffered with eczema more or less from birth. It's calmed down a lot now, but it was particularly bad during my teenage years. My mother, naturally concerned about me, took me to various dermatologists and other specialists. The blood tests showed that I was allergic to basically everything they tested me for, including rice, wheat, eggs, dairy, meat, and sugar. And so I was put on a special diet. I ate mostly different varieties of millet—"just like a little bird," as my mother used to say. These days, whenever I order couscous in a restaurant, I recall those millet days and feel strangely nostalgic. Needless to say, I couldn't eat any of the sweets sold in shops. That was tough, because as a child nothing on earth seemed more appealing.

Watching other children devour saccharine treats on the way back from school, I'd chew my fingers in envy.

When I was in high school, I stayed two weeks at a hospital in Kōchi Prefecture that had an excellent reputation for curing skin problems. Post-treatment, covered from head to toe in bandages, I had a taste of what it feels like to be a mummy. I can look back and laugh about it now, but at the time it was awful. Two or three years back, I happened to tell this story to an editor friend of mine and learned that she, too, had attended the same clinic as a teenager. We both marveled at the amazing coincidence, joked about being "mummy buddies," but the editor confided in me that it had been an agonizing time for her as well.

You might be thinking that compared to all the life-threatening illnesses out there, eczema is hardly a cause for complaint. Take it from me, though—it's excruciating.

Eczema means living with a constant sense of physical discomfort. It's very restricting when it comes to clothes, too, because you have to avoid any kind of synthetic fabric. At the school I went to, both the regular uniform and the gym clothes were made of polyester, so my mother spoke to the teachers and I got a special dispensation to wear a cotton blouse and PE outfit made from natural fibers. And although this is unrelated to the topic at hand, I can't help but mention how I have never forgiven the Japanese education system for forcing me to exercise in skimpy shorts. What shameful memories! But that's a subject for another day.

Women with eczema also need to be really careful with the makeup they choose. I'm happy to say that these days there's quite a range of organic cosmetics and skin products out there for those with sensitive skin, not to mention lots of lovely clothes made from skin-loving fabrics such as organic cotton and linen. I must admit that my career as a lifestyle essayist has definitely benefitted from catching on to this trend and pursuing it.

The hardest thing about eczema, acne, and other skin disorders is that you're always conscious of other people looking at you. People react instinctively to those who are different in some way. When my eczema was very bad, my classmates' eyes would inform me that I was a monster. That was why seeing Oiwa's and Okon's swollen faces on TV always made me sad. What had they done to deserve such a fate? Why did they have to be treated as monsters? In their plight I saw my own, and I pitied them.

Another thing about allergies is that they generally come in waves, going through good and bad phases, and that was definitely true of mine. In high school, this gave rise to a strange phenomenon. When my eczema flared up, none of the boys showed one iota of interest in me, but when my symptoms calmed down, I'd start being attractive to the opposite sex. I hadn't changed a bit on the inside, but when my eczema worsened the wave of boys would ebb, and when it got better, the tide would rush in. The numbers of girls who would talk to me traced a similar kind of graph. The whole thing felt totally absurd.

My eczema has given me keen observational skills. It has enabled me to see what the person I am talking to is really like underneath. Those who see others as monsters don't notice that those monsters are looking back at them in turn. When judging themselves superior, people are largely insensitive to the fact that they, too, are being judged. My observational eye serves me very well in my current job as an essayist. No doubt about it—it's my superpower.

Perhaps you're wondering why I'm bringing up superpowers now—and what exactly *is* a superpower, anyway? I should note at this point that I'm a die-hard French cinema fan (my all-time idols are Jane Birkin and Catherine Deneuve), but recently, in something of a departure from my usual habits, I went to see *The*

Avengers. My fourteen-year-old son (familiar to regular readers of this column) was desperate to go. Watching him as he stood there, self-assured and suave, with a bucket of caramel-coated popcorn in one hand and a Coke in the other, I was struck by how much he's grown. That said, once the film finished he was pestering me to buy him various bits of Avengers merchandise from the shop, so I guess he's still got some way to go!

Anyway, the film features various heroes with different superpowers, one of them played by Scarlett Johansson. And as I sat there watching them perform their many jaw-dropping stunts on screen, I started pondering what my own superpower was. Of course, I'm fully aware of how ridiculous it is to think about such things at my age. And yet, my dear readers, that was how I arrived at this tiny revelation. As it happens, I'm pretty content with my allotted superpower!

I'm aware that I've shown you a slightly different side of myself in this month's column, and I'd be lying if I said I wasn't a bit self-conscious about it. Now I'm really curious to hear what all your superpowers are! Don't be sheepish!

Drop me a line and let me know.

Until next month,

Kumiko Watanabe

Quite a Catch

Hina-chan has such beautiful skin, I think as I wash her. Using a linen washcloth I've specially ordered to avoid irritating her delicate skin cells, I start from her toes, working slowly up the length of her body stretched out supine in the water. When wet, the cloth molds itself perfectly to her smooth contours as if it were held there by some magnetic force.

The candle flame flickers as if trying to muscle in on our conversation, sending patches of shadow and light dancing across the bathroom walls.

I lift Hina-chan's right leg up a fraction. As my arm moves, the bathwater rocks and ripples, making little lapping sounds. My hand brushes the top of Hina-chan's thigh, and she lets out an embarrassed yelp, laughing and twisting her lower half away from me. We both know, of course, that this is just fooling around on her part—Hina-chan is fully accepting of the situation. With total composure, I clean each part of Hina-chan's body. This is a very important ritual for the two of us.

Perhaps there's a gust of wind outside, because the scent of flowers working its way through the high window grows stronger. Hina-chan flares her nostrils and drinks in the smell. As she does so, her flat little stomach arches upward, and my hand, which happens to be resting above her navel, feels it move.

"What kind of flower do you think that is?" she asks me.

"I wonder. I've never stopped to think about it." I tug at the chain of the plug to let out the bathwater, which is by now a sludgy brown, then say teasingly, "If you're curious, why don't you pop your head out and take a look? You're good at that, no?"

"It's the imagining that's the fun, silly. That's the problem with you, Shigemi-chan. No sense of adventure whatsoever." Hina-chan puffs out her cheeks, pretending to sulk. The water glugs its way down the drain.

"If I had to guess, I'd say camellia," I venture.

"Yes. Well, it's not a tulip, that's for sure."

"Wow, you're surprisingly clueless about flowers, aren't you?" I say, feigning outrage.

"You know what, Shigemi? That's what's called prejudice." Hina-chan wields her newly acquired piece of vocabulary with assured accuracy. She's a bright spark, that's for sure.

I rinse her down with the showerhead, and now her pearl-white skin comes into view. That glistening body of hers! Though I see it every day, it still has the power to amaze me every time. I reinsert the plug and turn on the tap so fresh water comes chugging through.

"Right!" Hina-chan says, as she passes her eyes proudly across her renewed body, free of mud. "Now, if the good lady would allow me the honor of massaging her feet . . ."

Sitting opposite each other in that smallish bathtub, Hina-chan's face is incredibly close to mine. Seeing her skin at such close range, so clear it seems almost translucent, still gives me the butterflies. She really is quite a stunner.

"You're so stiff! I guess that's the price you pay for working on your feet, you poor thing," Hina-chan coos as she kneads my soles. Beneath her deft fingers,

I feel the fatigue that has built up in my feet over the course of the day simply fall away, as if it had never really been there in the first place.

"This water smells really nice," Hina-chan says.

"Yeah, it's lavender bath milk."

"La-ven-dur-barth-mulk?" Hina-chan pulls a strange face, but it is obvious that she's gone and added a new word to her internal dictionary. By tomorrow, I've no doubt she'll be using it perfectly.

Until I met Hina-chan, I had no interest in bath milk, and I never really spent much time wallowing in the bath either. I went about carrying with me the fatigue I had amassed throughout the week. It was only after meeting Hina-chan that this small bathroom, whose uniformly cream-colored surfaces I had initially found rather depressing, became my favorite place to be.

My lover comes to me at night. Come rain, come gale-force wind, Hina-chan turns up on my doorstep every evening wearing the sunniest of smiles. Even if I'm utterly worn out, or if there's been some trouble at work and I am fed up with everything, I perk up as soon as Hina-chan arrives. She's my sun, my rainbow, my ray of light—she is every light source in the world rolled into one. Not to mention every source of loveliness and wondrousness too. We bathe together, eat dinner together, and fall asleep together. Then, when I wake up in the morning, Hina-chan is gone.

I get out of bed and pass my hand over the cold patch next to me, where not long ago Hina-chan was sleeping, her face the face of an angel. I give the sheets a shake to smooth the creases, fix myself breakfast, then head out to work.

Hina-chan worries that I'm not taking proper care of myself in the hours we're apart, so since our courtship began I've started living more healthily. Rather than buying my lunch from the convenience store, which inevitably means getting by on soggy pasta or rice balls shaped into triangles by machines rather than hands, I've started taking my own lunch boxes in as often as I can. It feels to me as if the badly formed omelettes and grilled salmon fillets and florets of steamed broccoli I make at home to bring to the office all contain Hina-chan's love. By eating my homemade food at work, I can be together with Hina-chan during the day too.

•

"Did you tell Yoshi about me yet?" Hina-chan asks now as she bores into a pressure point on the sole of my right foot.

"Didn't I tell you? Owowowowow!" I arch my back and try to flap my foot in pain, but Hina-chan keeps a tight grip on my calf, refusing to let go. Those tiny arms contain unknown reserves of strength. She flashes me a cheeky smile as if to say, *Do you have any idea who you're up against?* I'm pretty sure Hina-chan would be the most requested masseuse at any salon in town.

Yoshi is my next-door neighbor, a single guy in his late thirties. Before I met Hina-chan, he and I would occasionally go drinking in one of the cheap iza-kaya in town—two singletons whiling away the time, talking about nothing of significance. After breaking up with my then-boyfriend, I had crawled into life in my current apartment like some bedraggled survivor of a natural disaster, and Yoshi had done more or less the same—or the opposite, depending on how you looked at it. I was sick and tired of men; he was sick and tired of women.

Living with that boyfriend, my exhaustion had kept growing. He was a perfectly decent guy, and it wasn't like we argued all the time or anything, but sharing that cramped space with a creature so inflexible in both body and mind, and changing my existence to fit in with his being, wore me out like nothing else. Cohabiting with a man, I felt my body growing heavier, and I stopped acting on my own initiative. Instead, I would watch him, trying to gauge what move he was going to make next, or what he thought about things. It felt like I was accumulating a mound of pebbles inside me. In principle, the flat we'd shared was my home, but I always felt like I was in someone else's house. At some point, it dawned on me: I didn't want to live with another person. We broke up soon after that. So, when I met Hina-chan, I felt like patting myself on the back for the incredible luck that had befallen me.

One day not so long ago, as I was going about living my life—my wonderful, miraculous life now that Hina-chan was a part of it—Yoshi caught up with me by the communal mailboxes. Apparently, he'd clocked that something was going on from the voices that drifted through to his apartment each evening. And so, after he half-dragged me to one of the izakaya near the station, I told him all about Hina-chan, and how the whole thing had come about.

It all started, I told him, with a fishing outing—my

first ever. An old friend from school had invited me along, saying it would do me good to try something new, and so I'd found myself heading out on a day trip to the Tama River. My friend brought along all the gear.

For what seemed like an interminably long time I'd sat there, navy rod in my hands, staring at the surface of the river. Just as I was debating whether I'd waited for a catch long enough to be forgiven if I suggested giving up and heading home, I felt a tug. This is it, I thought, this is the part that's supposed to make it all worthwhile, and I began winding the reel around and around until the white thing dangling from the end of the line came into view. And, believe it or not, it was Hina-chan. Or rather, Hina-chan's skeleton. My friend promptly phoned the police, and they arrived to collect the corpse in no time. The tranquil riverbank where we'd been fishing just moments ago was instantly transformed into a foreboding crime scene.

Later, looking it up online, I found that Hina-chan's skeleton dated back a surprisingly long time, but nobody knew much else about it. They'd trawled the river for the bones missing from the skeleton but found zilch. They weren't even sure whether to treat it as a criminal case. Hina-chan's skeleton wasn't deemed a significant artifact of cultural heritage or anything, so it was going to be kept in the storage chamber of some organization I'd never heard of, and whose obscure name spoke volumes about the fact that, really, nobody knew what to do with the thing. It seemed clear that, for all practical purposes, it had been abandoned. But anyway, the skeleton in the vault isn't really what matters here.

After I'd caught the skeleton, and both my friend and I had been interviewed by the police, we'd parted ways, laughing wryly about how our fishing trip had turned out. My friend said that in all her twenty years' fishing this was the first time anything like this had happened. To my surprise, she messaged me a few hours later, offering to take me fishing in another spot the following week. I quickly declined. Landing an entire skeleton as my first catch ever went beyond beginner's luck and belonged to an altogether different realm. All that bone-baiting had left me quite exhausted, so I sunk down onto my bed and fell asleep for a couple of hours, still dressed in my approximation of fishing attire. I was awoken by the sensation of something brushing against my shoulder.

"H-hello?" said a wavering voice. I opened my eyes

to see a woman in a kimono standing by the bed, covered in mud and looking right at me. I let out a shriek. The mud-caked woman held up her hand in what seemed intended to be a reassuring gesture.

"I have come to thank you for earlier," she said.

"Huh?"

"Until today, I lay buried in the depths of the Tama River. Owing to your kindness I have once again seen the light of day, and I felt I couldn't possibly rest until I had offered my gratitude to you."

She must be talking about fishing out that skeleton, I thought. But . . . did this mean what I thought it meant? Was this figure standing in front of me dripping mud on my floor some kind of phantom? I somehow managed to restrain my impulse to leap up and scream.

Instead I waved my hand in an attempt at staying cool and said, "Oh, it was total coincidence. Don't even think about it. I was just in the right place at the right time."

"Please be so good as to listen to what I have to say. We shall be traveling back in time a couple of hundred years, to the Edo period."

"The Edo period . . . ?"

And just like that, she began to tell me about her

life. You know how in period dramas and TV programs from way back when, one of the characters launches into the story of their entire life? Well, it was just like that.

"That's right. After losing both my mother and my father to a terrible disease sweeping our village at the time, a relative attempted to marry me off to a certain gentleman, whom I did not desire to marry. When I stated my refusal in no uncertain terms, the gentleman took it upon himself to end my life, and then hurled my body into the river. Ever since, I lay outstretched on the riverbed, undiscovered by a single soul. As the months and days passed, many of my bones were swept away to heaven knows where."

"What? But that's awful! That's . . . that's completely unacceptable!"

I started to feel unbearably sorry for this ghost standing in front of me. What a bastard that guy was! I mean, he should've been locked up! And that relative of hers, too! Fuck! Marriage lasts a lifetime; it's not just something you can foist on people like that. You have to start considering other people's feelings a bit more.

"Well, yes, but . . ." Seeing my eyes widening in horror, the ghost lady tilted her head to one side, looking a little pained. Then she went on. "Well, anyway, that is what happened, and that is why I have come to thank you. It would be a great honor if you would let me serve you, as your chambermaid."

"My chambermaid . . . ?"

I didn't really know what she was going on about, but I knew that the present situation was untenable. I had the woman strip off her tattered, muddied kimono and then, seeing that her body was equally filthy, I decided to escort her to the bathroom and wash her down. When I picked up her kimono and saw the great gash running down the length of its back, I shook with anger. "Die, you samurai moron!" I hissed. "Yeah, you! I know you're already dead, but I want you to die again! Painfully!" It seemed like the greatest injustice in the world that a guy that evil was peaceably dead already.

"What's your name?" I asked the woman as I lathered up her hair. She bowed her head, as if she felt embarrassed to have so much attention lavished on her. There were great clumps of dirt enmeshed in her locks, and it was no mean feat to get them out. *This is all your fault, you stupid fucking samurai. If you've been reincarnated then hurry the fuck up and die now, in your contemporary incarnation.*

"My name is Hina."

"Hina-chan? Wow, that's a nice name. I'm Shigemi. People often tell me it's kind of old-fashioned."

"Lady Shigemi."

"Oh, Shigemi-chan is just fine."

"Right . . . Shigemi-chan . . ."

When I think back now to those first hours Hina-chan and I spent together, I explained to Yoshi, I feel ticklish with self-consciousness and pleasure. How awkward and faltering it all was! Hardly knowing a thing about each other, we both tried in our own way to get acquainted—just thinking about it brings tears to my eyes. What a beautiful thing it is when love begins to blossom.

"So basically, you're telling me you fished a skeleton from the river, and then a ghost appeared?" Yoshi summarized bluntly.

Yeah, I know what you're thinking. He who speaks of ghosts and expects to be believed is nought but a fool, and all that. But the truth was, my love for Hina-chan had taken away any fear I might previously have had about what Yoshi might say on the matter.

"Not just any old ghost, you know. Hina-chan's smart, and she's incredibly sexy. She's amazing."

I puffed myself up as if to say, *I'm not to be made fun of.* Then I picked up my mug of chūhai and downed it.

He who speaks of love must do so with courage. My attitude had to say, *If you're not going to believe me, then begone!*

"Well, it sounds like you've found yourself quite the girlfriend."

Maybe Yoshi was too drunk to care about the truth of my claims, or maybe he never had any intention of believing me, but in any case, he didn't challenge a single thing I said. He simply went along with it.

"Yep, she's really something." I felt immensely proud. It was all true, after all. Hina-chan really was incredible.

"I wish I could find myself a woman like that." Saying that, Yoshi slumped his head on the table.

He took off his glasses and wiped his eyes with the moist hand towel. Without his glasses, Yoshi immediately became more anonymous-looking. He kind of reminded me of the noppera-bō, the faceless ghost from old stories. Each time I saw this faceless face of his, I felt a twinge of guilt, as if I'd glimpsed something I shouldn't have. Here was a man born to wear glasses if anyone was. He'd once confided to me that when he took his glasses off to have sex, the other person would look at him suspiciously as if to say,

Who the hell is this guy? I could imagine that to be the case. Not that it really mattered to me one way or another.

"Well then, maybe you should try fishing too!" I said. "Although I mean, what happened with me and Hina-chan was pure fate. I really can't imagine that happening very often."

"So you see, I was boasting about you," I tell Hina-chan now. "But imagine if Yoshi has actually taken up fishing after that! That would make him a prize idiot."

Hina-chan smirks and nods, then makes a start on my left foot. She's humming what sounds like Beyoncé—who knows where she picked that one up. She has quite a sense of rhythm! Hina-chan has smashed all the preconceptions I ever had about ghosts. In fact, she somehow manages to surprise me every single day.

"If your life story was made into a book, it'd be a hard-boiled detective novel, don't you think?" I say to her. "It's got elements of science fiction, too. And horror, come to think of it, and fantasy . . . It's like the best story ever."

"Whereas yours would be like the biography of a withered old carrot. Yawns from beginning to end."

"Hahaha."

"Hehehehe."

Our laughs echo around the bathroom, wrapping around us and turning the bathroom into a surround-sound amphitheater.

"Okay, that's your massage done."

Hina-chan claps her hands together. We press our noses together and smile at each other.

Fresh out of the bath, dressed in an Adidas tracksuit, Hina-chan smells amazing. I've lectured her so many times by now that she has started to apply toner and lotion to her skin of her own accord. The look of intense concentration on her face as she dabs them on is pretty amusing. I think of it as my duty to ensure that Hina-chan's skin stays beautiful and pristine. Although having said that, the only time Hina-chan can move about at the moment is at night, so the chance of her suffering any kind of sun damage is pretty slim.

"I'm genuinely happy to wash you every day, you know?"

"Thanks, Shigemi-chan. I'm really sorry to be like this."

For some reason, Hina-chan's body is rebooted to its original form every day, so when she turns up at night, she's covered in muck again. Of late, she's taken to occasionally making her entrance with her arms dangling in front of her in a ghostly way, moaning, "I've come for youuuuuu!" I've no idea where she picked up that trick. When she sees me falling about laughing, though, Hina-chan looks very pleased with herself, and flashes me a grin.

My project at the moment is to somehow find a way of breaking into that vault in the research institute nobody's heard of, and smuggling out Hina-chan's skeleton so we can give it a proper memorial service. Hina-chan says that it doesn't bother her and I shouldn't worry about it, but it's something I'd really like to do for her. When I think about Hina-chan's skeleton cooped up all alone in some dark vault, I feel awful. I do worry that if I give the skeleton a proper memorial service, then Hina-chan will end up resting in peace forever and never visit again, but I guess if that happens, I can always just dig her up. There's no way I'd escape a haunting then. Hina-chan is totally cool with that plan too. "Lying there in the ground is too tedious," she says. "That's not my style."

At this moment, Hina-chan is lying on the sofa, her head resting on my knees and her eyes glued to the TV, munching away mindlessly at a bowl of avocado-flavored tortilla chips. I stroke her fine, silken hair, and think how deeply I adore her.

The Jealous Type

You are what they call "the possessive type." You're jealous in the extreme. The moment you sense something the slightest bit off in your husband's behavior, jealousy takes hold of you. When those green flames rage through your body, no one in this world can hold you back.

Your go-to strategy when seized by the feeling is to throw things. For the objects in your vicinity, it's an unmitigated disaster. You throw, and you throw, and you keep throwing.

If jealousy happens to strike in the bedroom, then you start with the pillows. First, your husband's. As you pick it up and cradle it in your arms, you find your chest flooded unexpectedly with a sweet memory from many moons ago: a school trip—you must have been fifteen or so, and you and the other girls in your class shared a big room at an inn, and when night fell, the great pillow fight got under way . . .

You lob your husband's pillow. That bedroom of yours has little space in it for anything other than the double bed, but still you swing your arm back and hurl it. It sails into the side of your husband's face, then plummets to the carpet. He doesn't retaliate like the girls at school. It's no fun for you at all. You try again with your own pillow, but your husband doesn't even attempt to catch it as it strikes his midsection, and then it, too, falls forsakenly to the floor.

The sight of those two pillows lying there on the carpet prompts you to the painful realization that the best years of your life were decades ago. Stuffed full with azuki beans, the pillows back at that inn had real heft to them and commanded quite some destructive force when thrown. You and the other girls had picked up those bean-filled pillows, their cases trimmed with lace and covered in little flowers, and hurled them at one another like bombs. You had rolled across the futons that covered the room's entire floor space with barely a crack in between, laughing until you had difficulty breathing. Strands of your hair found their way into your mouth, and your PE outfit got in a terrible tangle. Someone landed a direct hit to your face with a pillow, and you toppled over backward as the blood streamed from your nose, staining the offending pillowcase a vivid red.

These two pillows, though, utterly stationary on the floor, seem fundamentally different to those pillows of your adolescence. These two, stuffed with the perfect quantity of top-quality goose down, are as soft and fluffy as heaven itself. They were given to you as wedding presents and have your and your husband's initials embroidered in red and blue thread. When you throw them, they feel light and airy, as if they might just spread their wings and take off into the skies. In other words, you realize, they are no good for throwing at all!

Stupid old pillows. You have the same realization about them each time jealousy sends you on a throwing jag. You even get as far as thinking that tomorrow, you really must go out and buy some more solid pillows that can be weaponized, but as soon as your jealousy abates, you forget all about it.

Still disappointed by the pillows' lack of clout, you kick up each of your legs in turn, firing the slippers from your feet like two missiles, aimed right at your husband. As slipper toes go, these are on the more pointed end of the spectrum, so their landing isn't without effect. "Ow!" your husband says as one of the missiles strikes his shin. *I'll give you "ow," you bastard!* You are crazed, ablaze with jealousy, and your husband's little exclamation only stokes your fire further. You reach for the paperback on the bedside table and toss that in his direction. It's a flimsy little book, miserly in its lack of substance, and its impact is practically negligible—except it succeeds in informing your husband that you are still very much a resident of the green-eyed kingdom. You would be well advised to prepare for your next attack by keeping a hardcover tome by your bed at all times. Preferably some kind of encyclopedia. Two of them, even. Then you could pick up one in each hand and hurl them one after the other.

You swing back your arm and, with all the strength you possess, swipe at the row of photograph frames lining the top of the chest. Your wedding photo, the shot of the pair of you holding koalas on your honeymoon, along with all the other silver-framed special moments, skid along the wood, cascading off the side. A hard parquet floor would have produced a more audible crash, sure, but at least the plastic backs break and skitter dramatically across the carpet in fragments. Just look at the fear in your husband's eyes as he takes in those tiny shards.

With formidable determination, you cast an eye around the room in search of your next weapon of attack, but the bedroom really doesn't offer itself up as a plentiful arsenal. When lucid you're the tidy sort, and there's little that irks you more than a messy room. Plus, you read in a magazine article titled "How to Put Your Husband in the Mood" that getting rid of extraneous clutter helps men maintain focus in the bedroom, and since then you've been even more militant about keeping the room spick and span.

With no other options available to you, you make a lunge for your made-to-order curtains, howling like a wild beast—*GYAAAAAH!* You yank them down with all your might, ripping them from their rails. The light-resistant lining happens also to be flame-resistant, so there's no risk that your blazing jealousy will set them on fire. No sooner has curtain number one fallen with a muffled flop to the floor than you set upon the other. Your motions are exactly the same for curtain number two.

When it's all over, you stand there like Moses, a lone figure parting a sea of curtain. Your husband, who is cowering in the corner of the room, looks at you in astonishment. When you turn to meet his gaze, he looks away. The force of your jealousy hasn't dimmed in the slightest—and quite honestly, you'd like to keep going—but there's nothing here left for you to do; so from your curtain sea you let out a great wail. Resentful words spill out of you, and you sob and sob. When there are no suitable objects available, you have to make do by venting your emotions instead. The bedroom is not a prime location to be stricken by jealousy.

Unequivocally, the kitchen is the best place for jealousy to strike. When you are fortunate enough to be consumed there, you assume a look of positive radiance.

You start with the crockery you bought at the hundred-yen shop: the little white dishes with badly painted fish in royal blue, those ramen bowls everyone has seen at least once in their lives with the dragons encircling their circumference, the large plates decorated with eggplants and tomatoes. A mug whose sole distinguishing feature is its bright yellow hue. A voluptuous sake flask with a rough-textured glaze. Each time you go to the hundred-yen shop, you stock up on ceramics. They're all destined to end up in pieces anyway, so you don't even look at them, just sling them into your basket. Well-stocked is well-armed, after all.

You throw and you pitch and you chuck. You smash things to bits. Tiny particles of porcelain dance around you like a dust cloud. Sometimes they cut your arms and your legs, but what does that matter? You don't pay heed to such things, choosing to focus single-mindedly on your destructive activities. For you, such scars are the honorable wounds of a warrior. If anything, the scarlet blood adds a streak of color to your destruction, heightens the sense of drama.

When you've hurled the last of the hundred-yen crockery, it's time to take your bombardment to the next level. You dive into your medium-range selection: the dusky powder-blue stuff from IKEA, the items from MUJI's functional white series. Plates, tiny bowls, big bowls, teacups—you fling them all without distinction. You send them smashing down to the floor, regardless of whether or not they break. The lacquered wooden bowl bounces off the linoleum and rolls down the corridor, spinning around and around like a top.

Only your set of rapturously exquisite Noritake teacups will you not throw, not for anything. Those cost the earth, those cups. The ornate Arabian china is out of bounds, too. You collected those beauties one by one. They are your treasures, secreted away in the depths of your kitchen shelves. However potent the jealousy that overcomes you, you always retain at least that much presence of mind. In this world, there are things that are okay to throw and those that are not. On this point, your judgment is infallible. Your husband has curled himself into a ball under the table, shielding his head.

When you run out of things to throw, you tear off your polka-dotted apron and trample it. You plunge your fists down into the sink full of dishes with all your might, so the water goes splashing about you like great splatters of blood. You take some ice from the freezer, toss it into your mouth, and crunch down on it.

The kitchen's resources can always keep pace with the blazing fire of your jealousy.

You take up a large daikon and whirl it around you like a baseball bat. When you bring it crashing down on the table, the daikon—which must have been softer than you thought—breaks into pieces, like a slow-motion video. Doubtless you will use some of these in tonight's dinner—they're the perfect size for simmering. As you squeeze out every last drop of ink from a raw squid, you even have time to think that you'll combine the two, make ika-daikon.

Next, your eyes land on the cardboard box of apples that your parents sent over from their garden. You take them out and wrench them apart with your bare hands. Later you can make them into jam, or bake them in a pie, or mix them into macaroni salad—apples are surprisingly varied in their uses. You focus on channeling all your power into your fingers as they tear through the glossy skins.

Having destroyed the kitchen to the best of your ability, you begin to tidy up the mess strewn across the floor. When you tread on the miscellaneous shards, you can hear them screaming out in agony beneath your feet. You can empathize. The feelings of those little fragments are far easier to understand than those of your husband. Just because you're clearing up doesn't mean that it's over, mind. Your jealousy is still blazing wild and free, like the huge pyramid pyres at fire festivals.

You tidy like an incensed person, not missing a single piece. You clear up every last particle, however small. When you pick up your apron, you smooth out every crease. You refill the ice-cube tray so that the water in each hole is at exactly the right level, then put it back in the special compartment in the freezer. You compress the trash bag full of all the mess you created, then look again around the newly cleaned kitchen and breathe a sigh of relief. By this time, the lump of jealousy inside you has finally dissolved. The day you thought would never end has drawn to a close. You glance at your husband, still cowering under the kitchen table, and say with incredulity, "What on earth are you doing down there?" Then you start to hum a little tune.

The roots of your jealousy can be traced all the way back to your time at nursery school. At that early stage of life, your possessive nature was already in bud.

The first person you ever had a crush on was a male teacher, back in the days when it was still a rarity for men to have such a profession. That was a tough time for you. Whenever you saw this teacher picking up another child, a piercing grief would reverberate through your tiny body—the smaller the body, the quicker grief can race through it—and you would scream and cry. Needless to say, the teacher was more or less constantly cuddling other children and holding their hands, so you were more or less constantly in tears. By the end of the day, you were shattered.

When your mother came to pick you up, your teacher would report on the day, explaining that it seemed as if you were still missing your mommy. Hearing this, your mother was not altogether displeased. She'd stroke your hair and say, "Oh dear, oh dear!" As you looked up at the adults and listened to their conversation, the whole thing felt utterly unjust. Why couldn't they see you were genuinely in love?

At snack time, when your beloved would help other children eat, you would clench your fists so hard that the cookie in your hand was pulverized to a crumby mess. The verdict was that you "still lacked grip control."

At playtime, when your beloved erected magnificent building-block castles with the other children, you would let out a wail and charge straight into them, knocking them to the ground like a merciless god. As you lay there motionless on the floor, you could feel the scattered blocks lumpy beneath your body. It occurred to you that they were a bit like vegetable chunks, and the image of a bowl of vegetable-laden curry floated to your mind for a second, then disappeared.

At every stage of your development, your jealousy was remarkable. In grade school, you cast endless love spells from a book full of glitter-encrusted illustrations. When it dawned on you that they weren't working, you ripped the book to shreds. You tried your hand at black magic. You were never without a stock of voodoo dolls in your room. You visited a nearby shrine a hundred times to pray that the boy you were in love with would break up with his girlfriend. You stood naked under a waterfall and prayed with even more fervor.

When you fell for a boy in middle school, you stole his diary and kept it on your person at all times until you graduated. The heat of your body caused its cover to fade. You were assiduous in placing a curse on each and every girl you saw speaking to him. You worked with astonishing dedication in the hopes of getting into the same high school as him, so that in the end, you were admitted while he wasn't. Even once you were in your new school, the thought of all the girls he might be meeting was enough to make your blood boil over black. Ducking out after your last class, it was your daily afternoon ritual to walk over to his school and spy on him.

As a university student, your jealousy blossomed further still. When your boyfriend left a text of yours unanswered for five hours, the shock you endured made you come down with a fever. When the same boyfriend didn't pick up the phone, you would leave him voice mail after voice mail at two-minute intervals. That was no easy task, either—as soon as you put down the phone from recording one message, you'd redial to start recording the next. You were driven to such wild curiosity about his ex that you took an overnight bus to his hometown. When you approached and questioned the various people you met, you were mistaken for a private detective, and before long rumors were flying around that your boyfriend was mixed up in some bad business.

Your bible was *The Tale of Genji*. Every man you fell in love with, every man you went out with, caught a glimpse of hell. All of them, without exception. For the man that you married, every day was a living hell. Why'd he marry you, anyway? It was clear from the start what kind of person you were. When he casually checked the messages on his phone in your presence, hadn't he sensed your murderous gaze bearing down on him?

And what's more—and this is what's *really* amazing about you—until yesterday, you hadn't even realized that you were the jealous type. TV programs are always spilling over with crazily possessive girlfriends and wives, so you never questioned your normality. You were under the impression that this was what romance, what love was all about.

So what if jealousy had occasionally driven you to punch through the car window, or to rip to shreds the yukata you were sewing for your husband when it was inches away from being finished, or to slip a GPS device into his shoe to track his whereabouts? Even the way you were perpetually honing your sense of smell so that you'd instantly be able to catch a whiff of another woman on your husband's person seemed to you perfectly conventional behavior.

And so yesterday after dinner, when your husband announced that he wanted a divorce, quite out of the blue, your first reaction wasn't distress so much as utter bewilderment. He spoke at length about how abnormal he felt your jealousy was. It terrified him, he said, and he couldn't tolerate it anymore. It was sheer madness. Visibly teetering on the cusp of sanity, your husband sank his head onto the dining table like a Jenga tower tumbling down, and promptly dissolved into sobs.

You are a well-meaning person at heart, and so you were quickly overcome by deep regret. It had simply never crossed your mind until now that what you were doing was wrong. You apologized repeatedly to your husband, promised that you would change, and begged him for one more chance. Your husband smiled heroically. "Okay," he managed to squeak as he dried his eyes. Then, still somewhat ill at ease, the two of you sat in silence and ate the apple pie you'd baked for dessert.

Today you woke up feeling fresh and new. You felt rebirth was possible. You would become a kind-hearted person to whom jealousy was a foreign concept, a generous-spirited sort who could accept your husband just as he was. You swore to yourself that you would.

But—and here we reveal our real reason for getting in touch with you on this occasion—why on earth did you have to go and do something as banal as to *repent*? If your husband ignites the flames of your jealousy with the suspicious messages he receives on his phone, or the matchboxes he keeps in his pockets from dodgy-looking establishments, or the posh chocolates he brings home on Valentine's Day, then it's him that's in the wrong. If he makes you imagine he might have been unfaithful—leaving aside the question of whether he really is occasionally being unfaithful—then it is entirely his fault.

Why should you have to go and show benevolent forgiveness toward a husband like that? You made your dissatisfaction clear. Where's the problem with that? You've done nothing wrong. The misguided one here is your cheating husband. That's why, from now on, you should let yourself go wild with jealousy. We implore you not to part so readily with your defining asset.

Maybe you haven't realized it yet, but your jealousy is a talent. You mustn't go listening to the nonsense spouted by all the drudges surrounding you. They know nothing. There is no need for you to divest yourself of your own fangs. It would be the world's loss if you were to do so.

So long as your husband keeps up this flighty behavior of his, you should continue to show him hell. If he starts blathering on about divorce again, then find a chink in his armor and blackmail him. If necessary, we are happy to help you out in that regard by locating some kind of chink on your behalf. We don't think it will take long.

It is also testament to the singularity of your gift that your jealousy retains a youthful intensity even into your fifties. Ordinarily, individuals find their personalities softening as they get older. After living with someone for years on end, they develop a sense of resignation. Plainly put, they stop caring. Many women end up looking not to their husbands but to the male stars of their favorite TV programs to trigger their most passionate feelings. This is because such stars facilitate beautiful fantasies. There is nothing wrong with that, either.

Surely it has not escaped your notice how many married couples walk around with long-suffering expressions on their faces? Times change, but the path trodden by your standard married couple remains the same. You, on the other hand? You've never given up, not once. Your jealousy remains as fresh as a daisy. Even consulting our statistics, it's clear that your trajectory makes you a true outlier.

Barring any significant changes, we predict that the energy your jealousy generates will enable you to keep going strong until you are at least a hundred, but given that we are somewhat short of hands, we would prefer if you were to make your way here before then. The sooner the better, as far as we are concerned. The numbers of people with the levels of passion it takes to become a ghost are decreasing every year. Contrary to common presumption, it's not just anyone who can assume spectral form. Without the requisite degree of jealousy or obsession, people just float straight to heaven. Between you and us, everyone is so blessedly sensible that we sometimes find ourselves tempted to give them a good talking-to. *Are you really going to settle for that?* we want to ask. Quite frankly, watching over lives as dull as theirs, we are bored witless.

In today's world, there's a tendency for jealousy and obsession to be portrayed in a negative light. Those with talents in these areas are often criticized, as if they were lacking in some way. This only serves to ensure that people with extraordinary talent like yours shrink in number. This is the vicious cycle we find ourselves in. The situation is truly grave.

On that account, as embarrassing as it is to admit, we find ourselves chronically understaffed, and nothing would please us more than if you were to join our team. For a person of your gifts, we don't feel any training will be necessary and hope to welcome you into our team immediately. Recognizing your capabilities at this stage, we have extremely high expectations for what you could accomplish with us into the future. In terms of arrangements for your appearance on the spectral stage, rest assured that we have a wide variety of options available, and we feel confident that we'll be able to find something you will be satisfied with.

Accordingly, when you do pass away, please be sure to get in touch.

Where the
Wild Ladies Are

It was hands down the worst spring ever. Trudging wearily into the changing room, Shigeru wedged his shoulder bag inside his locker and, with a heavy heart, began to put on his coveralls. With no one else around, the room was totally silent.

Glancing up at the Seiko clock on the wall, Shigeru realized his shift was about to start. He'd been sure that he still had a good ten minutes to play with, but of late, time seemed to be wreaking havoc on him. Either that, or he was just zoning out too much. Shigeru kicked off his navy Converse and put on the black canvas shoes provided by the company. He left the room with his cap in hand, transferring it to his head as he navigated the dark corridors and the stairs as quickly as he could, finally turning into the room labeled MANUFACTURING ROOM NO. 6. When he reached his workstation, his manager, Mr. Tei, nodded at him in greeting. He had made it just in time.

Fresh out of university, Shigeru had quickly become what was colloquially termed a "flitter": someone who bunny-hopped from one fixed-term contract to another, without ever becoming a permanent employee. These days, with permanent positions becoming something of a rarity and companies taking on equal numbers of female employees, being a flitter had become more or less the norm, and the word was losing its original significance. Nonetheless, Shigeru still found the term appropriate for his current state. Both materially and spiritually speaking, he was a flitter.

Switching places with the morning-shift worker, Shigeru took up position at the end of the assembly line and commenced inspection. His work here was supremely easy. He simply had to watch the sticks of dried, compressed incense that went streaming past him down the conveyor belt, and check that they weren't misshapen or broken. The incense had a peculiar aroma, like nothing he'd ever smelled before. In the beginning, that weird smell pervading the entire working space got to him, but now he was pretty much used to it. More important, a job where he didn't have to use his brain was ideal for Shigeru in his present mental state.

One day last year, every last drop of Shigeru's motivation had evaporated all at once. It was the day his mom had killed herself. Shigeru had been the one to find her body after she'd hanged herself with a bath towel. His first reaction wasn't one of sadness, but perplexity—it was as if his mom were playing some kind of practical joke on him. She just wasn't the kind of person to go and do something like that. She was a hearty old thing; a ball of energy; a living, breathing stereotype of the Middle-Aged Woman Who Won't Shut Up. But it wasn't a joke. His mom really and truly was dead.

At the wake before the funeral, Shigeru had seen Okumura for the first time in what seemed like ages. Okumura had been his mom's lover for years, and, biologically speaking, was Shigeru's father. Shigeru had seen a fair bit of Okumura while he'd been in grade school, but by the time he reached his mid-teens, it had become clear they didn't have much in common. In any case, Shigeru had never really thought of Okumura as his dad—he was just some guy who came around a lot, and who seemed to like spending time with his mom. His mom was cheerful as it was, but when Okumura came over, she grew even brighter, so Shigeru supposed he couldn't be a bad sort. Instead of looking at Okumura directly, Shigeru would look at the way that his mom looked at Okumura. That captured his attention more profoundly.

When Shigeru was little, Okumura would always show up at the house with a present for him: plastic models of planes and tanks, or baseball gloves and balls, or what have you. He never played catch with Shigeru, though—he merely presented him with the gear. Okumura didn't look like the type to play baseball, anyway.

One time, when Shigeru opened up the flat rigid parcel that Okumura handed him, he found a picture book inside. The title read *Where the Wild Things Are*, and the cover illustration showed a horned monster fast asleep in a seated posture, with a sailboat in the background.

Okumura and his mom were sitting together, drinking and chatting. Shigeru flopped down on the floor in a spot where he could be seen and began to leaf through the book. He thought that doing so would make his mom happy. The TV was blasting out a popular variety show. The summery evening breeze that slipped in through the open window was musty and warm. Shigeru's feet were bare, just like the monster's on the cover of the book.

The main character in *Where the Wild Things Are* was called Max, a boy of about Shigeru's age. Max got in a sailboat and sailed for a year and a day, until he reached the place where the wild things were. Then Max got to dance and play with the wild things. The wild things in this book hadn't been made kid-friendly or cute. They were huge, and they looked properly scary. Shigeru liked that. They had pointy fangs and claws, and staring, goggly eyes. They were pretty cool.

At the end, when Max made to go home, the wild things said to him, "Oh, please don't go—we'll eat you up—we love you so!"

Aghast, Shigeru looked up from the page toward his mom. Her cheeks were flushed, and she was laughing at something Okumura had said. Her expression somehow became one in Shigeru's mind with the words in the picture book he'd just read: "I'll eat you up—I love you so!" Then Shigeru looked at Okumura's face. "I'll eat you up—I love you so!" He looked every bit as happy as Shigeru's mom did.

At the wake, the now-gray-haired Okumura made no attempt to conceal his grief. Raising his head from Shigeru's mom's coffin, he came right up to his son, tears and snot coursing down his face. Before stopping to think it might be rude to do so, Shigeru found himself backing away in fear until his shoulders brushed up against the black-and-white-striped banners hung on the wall, and he could go no farther. With no hesitation, Okumura took both of Shigeru's dry hands in his and squeezed them tight.

If one were to give a summary of the incoherent, sob-punctuated rambling that ensued for the next five minutes, it would go something like: "I'm sorry," "I'm truly sorry," "I'll make sure you're taken care of until you graduate," "I'm sorry from the very bottom of my heart." Last of all, Okumura said, "There are times when something that is more important to you than you ever knew, more meaningful than you ever thought, is torn out of your hands and carried so far away that you can never get it back." He let his shoulders slump, patted Shigeru's hand a few times, patted Shigeru's shoulders a few times, and then shuffled away with little tiny steps, like a man who'd lost all hope. Watching Okumura as he walked away, it struck Shigeru that people could just burn out. They got old and they burned out. But then, Shigeru was in his early twenties and he was just as burned out as Okumura was. He didn't feel any particular desire to shout at Okumura. Shigeru stood in the corner of the room all night, watching the adults as they cried and shouted and blew off steam however they felt like it.

The timing was unfortunate, to say the least: all of this took place in Shigeru's third year of university when he was supposed to be venturing out into the turbulent sea of job-hunting. Shigeru felt barely capable of surviving a gentle wave lapping up on shore, let alone a turbulent sea. Between him and a sand castle built by a kid with a plastic spade, Shigeru suspected he'd be the first to collapse.

He had gone along with his cohorts to a job-hunting seminar held in one of those big lecture halls, but as he listened to the speakers going on about how to keep up one's motivation and fill in "winning" application forms, he realized that all this was impossible for him, and left the room. Just being around all that positivity left him mentally drained.

Shigeru had sat down on a sun-bleached wooden bench in the courtyard and drunk a can of coffee as he waited for his friends to emerge from the lecture hall. He had no motivation, no energy, and no desire to apply himself. The idea of presenting his "achievements" in the best possible light on an application form seemed like the greatest torment imaginable. Why did you have to sell yourself, to fill out a stupid application form, to start working? There was just no way he could do that.

Now, watching the convoy of little sticks gliding past in the factory where he worked, Shigeru thought about the incense holders that stood both at his mom's altar and beside her grave. Since his mom had died, Shigeru would light a stick of incense at their home altar every day without fail, and he visited her grave with great regularity. In the graveyard, Shigeru felt calm. As long as he was there, he could believe that his mom, who had vanished so abruptly, was actually with him, beneath that stone slab.

Sometimes, when Shigeru was standing in front of his mom's grave, he would hear the faint strains of a song. He would all look around him, but invariably he was the only one there. He found it a bit spooky, for sure, but he figured it must be some big, elaborate family grave with a built-in stereo. Who needed a feature like that in a gravestone, though? It irritated

Shigeru to have his few moments of peace interrupted in that way.

Before his mom's death, Shigeru had been seeing a girl from his year, but after the event, she immediately began to distance herself from him, as if his despondency might be infectious. Such a thing couldn't be helped, Shigeru thought. He understood as well as anybody that if you fell prey to a negative state of mind, you became incapable of believing in a future where you could thrive. In place of the requisite hope, Shigeru now felt only despair.

In fact, the only person who wanted anything to do with him since his mom's death was his cousin. She had suddenly begun calling and emailing, telling him that she didn't think his frequent grave visits were making his mom happy. When Shigeru asked her what her reasoning was, the cousin would fall silent, and then come out with some idiotic response like, "I dunno, I just kind of get that vibe, you know?" He sensed that she'd changed considerably of late. Previously she'd lacked confidence and was forever putting out feelers to the people around her to gauge what they were thinking, but these days she gave out an almost authoritative aura, as if to signal that she couldn't care less what other people made of her. It was like she'd become invincible.

From where he stood behind Shigeru, Mr. Tei reached out and plucked a single stick of incense from the production line. Shigeru couldn't see any problems with its shape or color. Noticing Shigeru peering at him with curiosity, Mr. Tei gave him a blank nod, then walked off to assess the next production stage. Mr. Tei, who wore black-framed glasses and appeared to be in his early thirties, seemed utterly inscrutable to Shigeru. Even his nods failed to reassure Shigeru. There was something far too cryptic about them.

Despite Shigeru's perennially vacant state of mind, it had begun to dawn on him that there were some slightly odd aspects to the incense production process. For starters, the first stage, where fragrant oils were blended with plant materials, took place in the adjoining room and was kept secret from other employees. In-house secrets were not a rarity, but the few times Shigeru had stolen a glimpse of what was going on in there, it had looked genuinely weird. There were always two elderly women standing there, and on occasion he had heard them chanting, as if reciting a spell. Initially he assumed they were just chatting with each other, albeit in a rather strange fashion, but the longer he looked, the more certain he was that they really were addressing the large pot in which the ingredients were mixed together. However long he stayed out there listening, he couldn't understand a single word of what they were saying. Also, why were the women in that room always in kimonos? The sashes wound around their shoulders to hoist up their sleeves gave them an air of intense dedication—a far cry from the slapdash impression of Shigeru in his uniform.

The thoroughly blended incense mix was then carried from the secret room to Manufacturing Room No. 6, where Shigeru and his colleagues worked, and fed into a machine that resembled a noodle maker, and which shaped and cut the wet mix into small rod-shaped pieces. By the time these reached Shigeru's section of the line, the sticks would be completely dry. That he found quite mysterious, too. Surely incense should, in theory, take a good twenty-four hours to dry out? Sometimes, he'd catch the person overseeing the post-cutting production stage waving a hand over the slender sticks. Was there some kind of secret to be revealed there, too?

Truth be told, this whole company was something of a mystery to Shigeru. He'd applied for the job after seeing it advertised in a free local employment paper he'd picked up at the convenience store. Some of the words cramped in the tiny square notice had been so blurred that he could barely make them out, so it was hard to tell what kind of company it was, or the exact nature of the work. The only thing he could see for certain was that the hourly rate was on the higher side. Shigeru had assumed his vision must be deteriorating. Not only that, but as he headed to the interview, he was seized by panic upon realizing he couldn't for the life of him recall the company's name.

There were three people interviewing him that day. On the left sat Mr. Tei, dressed in a suit rather than his usual work gear. The person in the middle, the eldest on the panel, told Shigeru that the company manufactured a wide variety of products and offered a range of different services, explaining that he might need to move frequently between departments. Would he mind that? "No, not at all," Shigeru had answered. In his heart, of course, he was saying, *Whatever, I really couldn't care less!*

Mr. Tei had called to inform him he'd gotten the job.

As soon as Shigeru started work it became clear to him that the company was full of middle-aged women. Young men like Shigeru were few and far between. In the first few days, he briefly worried that the women might all start cooing over him as if he were some kind of celebrity, vying for his attention and getting into fights over him, but he soon realized he had no need to fear on that count. The women didn't treat him as a foreign presence—indeed, they showed no particular interest in him whatsoever, though they were kind to him in their own way.

Shigeru discovered that being surrounded by women indifferent to his presence made everything pleasantly uncomplicated. He struggled considerably more around Mr. Tei, who was closest to him in age, and toward whom Shigeru couldn't help but feel a sense of male solidarity. Not that Mr. Tei paid Shigeru any particular attention. When addressing Shigeru, his face remained as expressionless as it did with everyone else. The women in the company seemed to respect Mr. Tei, and would frequently go up and speak to him, apparently unfazed by his lack of social graces. There was no doubting his popularity.

The building turned out to be unexpectedly cavernous, in a way that Shigeru never would have predicted on first seeing its small, unassuming entrance. The company really did make a miscellany of products, and the manufacturing rooms numbered in the dozens, although the precise number fluctuated on a daily basis, and sometimes Shigeru got the feeling that a staircase or a room he'd never seen before had materialized before his eyes. At those times, though, he'd tell himself that he was still new to the building, and just hadn't got a proper grasp of its architecture yet. In Shigeru's current state, none of that stuff really affected him much, anyway. When he went outside, the cherry trees lining the main road were in full bloom, obscuring the contours of the world even further. And for Shigeru's heart, blurry, ambiguous things were the easiest to bear. He had almost no contact with his university friends who'd now embarked on their new lives. Any hint of peppiness or positivity in their words felt like a stab in Shigeru's chest. He wanted to minimize the damage that the future was going to deliver him.

Coming and going between home and work, the days passed by uneventfully.

On one of his days off, Shigeru was tidying his mom's grave as usual when he heard the singing again, this time much more clearly. No doubt the volume control on that stupid singing grave had broken, Shigeru thought. He strained his ears in irritation. He had an impulse to locate exactly where the sound was coming from and break the idiotic thing. The voice crooned:

> *Please, oh please, my dear,*
> *Please don't go crying by my graaave.*
> *I'm not in there, you hear,*
> *I'm not sleeping at all.*

Shigeru was flabbergasted. He knew this song! It had been a big hit! He and his mom had watched that tenor perform it as part of the Kōhaku song contest, which was on TV every New Year's Eve. He could remember his mom munching on a rice cracker as she cooed, "Ooh, I like this one."

But surely, in terms of songs to play in a cemetery, this was about the most inappropriate choice ever. The voice began again, now repeating the same phrase over and over.

> *I'm not in there, you hear!*
> *I'm not in there, you hear!*
> *I'm not in there, you hear!*

It came to Shigeru like a bolt: it was his mom's voice! And then, as if it had noticed Shigeru's noticing, the voice fell quiet. However intently he listened, Shigeru could no longer hear anything, not even the sound of the wind. He was standing there all alone, in complete silence.

Today, as always, an endless procession of incense sticks was gliding past Shigeru's eyes. The sticks that passed inspection would be boxed, wrapped in paper with the words SOUL SUMMONER brushed on in ink, and taken to the shops. Shigeru didn't know what effect the incense was supposed to have, but he knew it was one of the company's most popular products. At lunch the other day, he'd asked the women there about it, but they'd giggled and avoided answering the question. Shoveling down his katsu curry, Shigeru then asked the other question that had been on his mind.

"Don't you think this company's a bit weird sometimes?"

By now, Shigeru had recovered enough of his mental equilibrium to be able to perceive when something was a bit off. He'd cut back on his graveyard visits, going only every other week. However much he strained his ears, he couldn't hear the singing anymore these days. He got the sense that maybe, if he greatly increased the number of his visits, he might be able to hear it again—but he also knew that doing so would upset his mom.

"Well, companies *are* weird, aren't they," one of the ladies said after a pause, as she gobbled up the broad strip of deep-fried tofu sitting on top of her kitsune udon. Her slanted eyes and narrow face had a vulpine quality to them, Shigeru noted. And come to think of it, weren't the kitsune—the fox spirits capable of transforming themselves into humans—supposed to love deep-fried tofu above all other foods? Wasn't that, in fact, where the dish had got its name? But he brushed off these thoughts as quickly as they had come to him.

"No, that's not what I mean," he continued hesitantly, but the women tittered and quickly steered the conversation to the new bakery that had opened up by the station, and whose head pastry chef had allegedly trained in France.

"The savarin is to die for!"

"Oh, but not a patch on the Mont Blanc!"

"I've never been. Is it really that good?"

"I'm fairly sure they use only proper butter, not margarine. My gosh, you can taste the difference!"

As Shigeru listened to the conversation unfolding

around him, his jaw hanging open, one of the women, with an unusually large mouth, offered to pour him a cup of green tea from the thermos on the table. As she poured, some of the steaming liquid splashed across her arm, but she didn't bat an eyelid. From the enormous pouch that she carried around with her, the vulpine woman brought out some individually wrapped custard-filled cakes, and everyone at the table let out squeals of joy.

What a peculiar place I've ended up in, Shigeru thought to himself.

Loved One

People are always so surprised when I say I don't know what osmanthus smells like, but I do have my reasons. I've suffered from rhinitis since I was little, and distinguishing smells is not my strong suit.

Come autumn, fellow pedestrians will occasionally stop still in the middle of the pavement or while turning a corner, and say, their tone suddenly lightening, "Oh, osmanthus! How lovely!" It wears me down to explain each and every time how I used to pay frequent visits to the Ear, Nose, and Throat Hospital when I was younger to try to sort out my rhinitis—to explain that with the pointy machine they stuck up my nose, its weird and repetitive buzzing as it sucked up the mucus, and the strange sensation this provoked, I eventually got fed up with the endless hospital visits and stopped going—and since then, have just been making do with over-the-counter drugs. So when people go on and on about the fragrance of osmanthus, I sometimes pretend to understand what they're talking about and agree with them, although really I don't have the foggiest idea what sets it apart. At these times, the only thing I'm really marveling at is how popular this osmanthus scent seems to be. On the rare occasion when I confess that I have no idea how it smells, people react as if I'm some hard-hearted brute. Other flowers don't seem to provoke such a violent reaction, so I assume osmanthus must be special in some way.

I've even met people who've said they wished there were a perfume that smelled like osmanthus. Perfume isn't really my area of expertise either, obviously. I've never bought a single bottle of the stuff. Once or twice, I've tried out perfumes that people have given me, but it felt stupid to be walking around wearing a fragrance that I myself couldn't smell, so I stopped.

When you have no sense of smell, you can rule out a lot of options in life. For example, I have zero interest in aromatherapy or incense, which are all the rage now. Magazines and commercials agree that incorporating such products into your daily routine has a healing effect and facilitates a more relaxed way of living, which makes me think that maybe I've missed out entirely on the experience of being healed. What does it feel like, I wonder, to be healed like that?

But now I can see it's a good thing that I've bypassed all of that fragrance stuff. I realized that just the other day when I stumbled across an article online about how aromatherapy can be harmful to cats. As it happens, I never once used aroma oils or anything like that around the house when Tortie was alive, but if my nose had functioned normally and I hadn't known about the effect of oils on cats, then I may well have. In general, I'm not that reliant on the internet, but I do think it's useful sometimes. It was through the internet that I found out that the smell of mint can have an adverse effect on cats, too. But thanks to my nose problems, fragrant plants have never had a place in my life either. What fortune!

Not that I'm fortunate all the time, of course. Recently, I came down with a cold although it really isn't the cold season, and while I was tucked up in bed recovering, the supply of incense for the home altar ran out. Reluctant to go out shopping when I was feeling under the weather, I went into my dad's room for the first time in ages and managed to root out some old incense in one of his drawers. His room is basically as it was when he died. Anyway, it was scented incense that I found, not the kind you're supposed to burn on altars, but I decided to use it anyhow. I know people are funny about that stuff, but it doesn't bother me too much. Probably something to do with my reduced olfactory capabilities. Without fragrance to go on, there's not much to differentiate between incense for altars and the regular kind. They're all thin little lines that launch other thin little lines into the air, as though they're trying to grow taller. Incense smoke always looks to me like a soul emerging from a body. A weakling soul. From time to time, I reach out and try to stroke those weakling souls, but they always slip through my fingers, rise higher, and then disappear. Where do souls go after they've disappeared, I wonder?

Anyway, I didn't really see any problem with my incense repurposing, so I kept on using on the altar the stuff I'd found in my dad's drawer. I guess you could call me sloppy in that regard. I didn't know how old it was, but there was about half of it left in the box.

I recovered from my cold soon enough and had resumed my habit of stopping at the nearby shopping arcade on a daily basis—but even when I passed by shops selling altar incense, I'd think, well, I still have that other stuff left over—and then I'd just keep walking. I was more interested in the asparagus on sale for eighty-eight yen a bunch.

One day, as usual, I lit a stick of incense on the altar and was just starting to fold up my washing when I heard someone say in a pained voice, "Ermm, I'm sorry to bother you. I can see you're busy."

The voice had a confident, solid timbre. Assuming that some guy collecting money or soliciting for something or other had made his way up to the house through the front garden, I looked over to the window, but there was no one there.

"Oh, sorry. I'm over by the altar."

I turned my head and, sure enough, right by the altar was a man wearing a suit and black-framed glasses, floating in midair. I was sitting down on the tatami, so I was saved the trouble of falling on my backside in shock. I looked up at the floating man in amazement.

"Please don't be alarmed, madam. I'm not a ghost. I'm here on business, from the incense company."

My eyes scanned his body before falling on a name

tag pinned to his chest. The tag had a single, rather unusual character printed on it.

"Mr., eh, Migiwa?" I asked hesitantly. It wasn't a name I'd ever seen before.

"Ah, no, it's Tei." Aha, I thought, a Chinese name. That made sense. I'd thought there was something a little bit idiosyncratic about his intonation.

"Ah, Mr. Tei. Your Japanese is very good."

"Yes, well," he said blankly, then continued. "In ordinary circumstances I'd offer you my business card, but these circumstances prevent my doing so . . . I hope you'll forgive my impertinence."

I found it utterly bizarre to be addressed with such extreme politeness by a figure who'd literally come floating out of my altar, but I decided not to dwell on it.

"I am here to speak to you about this product of ours that you're using. It appears that you still haven't been experiencing its effect."

"Its effect?"

"Yes. It doesn't always work perfectly, but for the most part, people can expect to start seeing their loved one as they were during their lifetime within a week or two."

"Huh? Is that what this incense is for?" I could barely believe what he was saying.

"Yes, indeed. I don't believe that the batch in your possession is defective in any way, so I decided to pay you a visit, to find out if there was some issue preventing it from taking effect. I was wondering if you'd be able to provide me with the name of your preferred loved one, so we can make the necessary adjustments from our side? These days, of course, with online customer reviews having so much sway, we do all we can to see to each and every one of our customers' needs."

Mr. Tei's expression was one of utmost seriousness. I ran his words through my mind: *my preferred loved one.* I supposed that, in theory, I should nominate one of my parents, but the truth was that if either of them were to come back now, I wouldn't really know what to say. This was especially true of my dad, even though— what with my mom dying when I was very small—I'd grown up around him. If anything, it felt like I'd spent too long a time in this house with that mute creature. Even now that he was dead, I didn't feel entirely alone. I could sense his muted presence around the house. There weren't many other options either. I'd dated people when I was younger and stuff, but I'd never been married, and there wasn't anyone for whom I harbored any particularly strong feelings. Then I remembered the other mute creature that had once lived with me.

"It's Tortie," I said.

"Tortie?" Mr. Tei's tone sounded a little quizzical, but his face remained unchanged. He was what you might call an expressionless person, but his voice had a soft quality to it, and I found it very calming to listen to.

"Yes, Tortie. My cat. I got her when I was in my late twenties, and she lived to the grand old age of nineteen. She was here with me after my father died." Having no sense of smell, I'd never had the experience of being healed by a particular scent, but I feel like for those nineteen years, Tortie had performed the same function for me. Time and time again, I'd been healed by the softness of her fur, the way she would leap up onto my shoulders or my lap, the mewling sound she made that was just so very *catlike*, the sight of her gazing out of the window, how she looked when she woke up—I was soothed by everything about her, in fact. Even after she started getting old and her health deteriorated, and I had to take her to the vet all the time and give her all sorts of medicines, she still soothed me. Tortie was a wonderful being. Maybe all cats are.

Looking slightly taken aback, Mr. Tei began speaking in a slightly more hurried manner.

"Goodness, yes, you're right. There really is no

justification for us to limit loved ones to human be-ings. It's a truly embarrassing oversight on our part, a bug in our system that we've been too shortsighted to recognize all this time. Please accept my sincere apol-ogies. I'll feed that back to our technical team right away. Can I ask you to wait one more week? I promise that you'll be able to see Tortie after that."

"Oh yes, of course."

All of this was most unexpected to me, but the prospect of being reunited with Tortie was a very pleasing one. Even if I couldn't actually touch her, I didn't mind. Just seeing her would be enough.

From his aerial position, Mr. Tei finished jotting down his notes, then looked at me. In the fixity of his stare, I could sense the passion with which he ap-proached his work.

"We also pay a lot of attention to the aroma of our products. In theory, the incense should be emitting your favorite smell, but for some reason it hasn't been able to pick up that data either. If you have a preferred fragrance, please do let me know."

"Oh, I'm not good with smells. I've got nose problems."

"Is that so?" A troubled look came over Mr. Tei's face.

"Yes. I don't even know what osmanthus smells like."

"Osmanthus . . . Well, personally I feel like osmanthus is not too far removed from the taste of loquats. It's a sweet smell, but not too sweet. Sort of fresh, with something slightly nostalgic about it," he said earnestly, with not the slightest hint of a smile.

The taste of loquats, I thought. For an instant, the area around my nostrils tingled, and I felt the premonition of a smell. Was this the smell of osmanthus? It was the first time anybody had ever explained a smell to me in words, and it came as something of a revelation. It turned out that you could use something you knew well as a guide to help you draw closer to something completely unknown! I stared unguardedly at Mr. Tei, but his face had resumed its usual blank expression.

"Okay, then. Can you make it smell of osmanthus?"

"You're sure?"

"Yes. Please."

"Very well. As I say, if I could ask you to wait just one more week, that would be much appreciated. Goodbye." Mr. Tei bowed politely, then vanished.

•

In the days that followed, I continued to use the incense. I looked it up on the internet and discovered that just as Mr. Tei had suggested, it was a pretty standard product, so if it ever ran out, I could always buy a new box. The fact that it had been in my father's room suggested that maybe he'd been using it to see my mother from time to time. It was endearing to think of him doing so every now and then, never once letting on to me about it.

In two days' time, it'll be a week since Mr. Tei's visit.

A Fox's Life

"If you were an animal, you'd definitely be a fox," the young man next to Kuzuha piped up out of the blue.

Kuzuha's eyes twinkled. "*If*, you say . . ."

Since she'd been a child, Kuzuha had been told she resembled a fox. There was something decidedly vulpine about her long, lithe body, not to mention her narrow eyes and slender face. She realized early on that "You look like a fox" wasn't intended as a compliment. Ironically, the girls held up as "foxy" at school were actually those who looked nothing like foxes.

In her twenties, when Kuzuha was working in an office, the nation was rocked by the Glico-Morinaga scandal, an extortion case that targeted several major confectionary companies through blackmail campaigns and kidnapping. The only known suspect from the mystery group calling itself "The Monster with 21 Faces" was identified in the papers as "the fox-eyed man." As his antics wreaked havoc on Japanese society, Kuzuha cursed him internally for giving foxes an even worse reputation than they already had. With their round eyes and tubby bodies, Kuzuha's parents were built more after the model of another shape-shifting animal, the tanuki, and Kuzuha's sister, older than her by five years, had been born one too. Kuzuha grew up as a lone fox surrounded by cuddly raccoon dogs.

The fox was good at school. From the very beginning, there wasn't a single subject that she struggled with. She excelled at sports, too.

Whenever she approached a problem, Kuzuha spotted a shortcut. These shortcuts were always immaculately paved, without even the tiniest of pebbles littering the surface; the arrow-straight path they traced to the answer was well lit. All Kuzuha had to do was waltz her way there. When her classmates complained of finding their schoolwork hard, Kuzuha simply couldn't understand what that was like.

Yet for all her mental agility, Kuzuha was incapable

of sitting back and enjoying her cleverness. Each time she performed well in a test and the results list stuck up in the classroom showed her name above all the boys', she felt everybody's eyes on her. Outshining the boys only made other people uncomfortable, and consequently, Kuzuha was troubled by a creeping feeling that something bad was going to happen to her. Sometimes she loathed that pebble-free, arrow-straight path. If only it had a few weeds, the odd twist and turn—something, Kuzuha thought. Then she could trip and fall in a cute, comical way, and other people would look and laugh, and she'd be able to laugh along with them. That was a more suitable way for a girl to be. Kuzuha loathed standing out. She couldn't see a single benefit to it. People resented girls and women who stood out, both in her class and in the world outside it. That was how it seemed to Kuzuha.

Kuzuha could see shortcuts, which meant she could also see what was to come. She knew that however hard she tried, the path ahead would always be blocked to her at some point. History proved it, society proved it, and various statistics proved it. As long as it was just her and her textbook, she could play with her shortcuts, but eventually Kuzuha's route would be sealed off entirely. She would have no hope of winning.

And if Kuzuha had to start out all over again when she came up against the blockage, she would have to take a very long way around indeed. Could anybody really blame Kuzuha for concluding that the most expedient shortcut was not to make any effort at all? That it was, in fact, wiser not to dream big and to become, instead, a person who didn't offend anyone? When the time came for Kuzuha's classmates to decide on their future plans, Kuzuha announced with the utmost composure that she was going to look for a job straight out of school. The teachers practically leaped from their chairs in shock. Uproar engulfed the staffroom.

In the Career Advice Room, and during several visits to Kuzuha's home, her teachers attempted time and time again to persuade Kuzuha and her parents that she would be better off continuing her education. "We are entering an age where women, too, will be attending university," the teachers prophesied, "and your daughter really is exceptionally gifted."

One time, the deputy head himself came out to speak with them. Kuzuha was astonished that she had elicited such a violent reaction from her teachers. Even her parents, who didn't oppose Kuzuha going to university but had intended to leave the decision up to her, seemed so stirred by the fuss being made that they began suggesting to their daughter that perhaps she really should go after all. But Kuzuha refused to listen. In the end, the lengthy discussions ended with her teachers and her parents all making the same vacuous statement:

"Well, I guess she is a girl, after all."

Yes, thought Kuzuha, you've got that right. I'm a girl after all, and that's just fine. From her seat beside her parents, Kuzuha observed the doleful look in her teachers' eyes with great perplexity.

Fast-forward, then, to Kuzuha's welcome party at her first job. She had found herself an administrative role at a local company.

"There's something foxlike about this one," said the department head at this new company, his reddened face glistening, as Kuzuha refilled his empty glass. He made no attempt to conceal the fact that he was sizing Kuzuha up, ogling her with his moist eyes. It was the first time Kuzuha had been looked at in that way. She sensed, with a feeling close to wonderment, that she had entered a new phase of her life, and vowed to remember this moment forever.

The welcome party was being held in a tatami

room they'd rented out for the occasion, on the first floor of a small Japanese restaurant. The long, narrow space was filled with sounds: sounds of men, sounds of women, sounds of tableware. Kuzuha felt astonished that a group of fully grown adults could produce such an almighty racket, but she took care not to let her astonishment show.

"Yes, I'm often told that," Kuzuha said with a cheerful smile. Encouraged, the department head placed his hand on Kuzuha's stockinged knee. Kuzuha felt nothing—neither pleasure nor discomfort. She found it genuinely bizarre that he would want to touch her that much, but that was it. Huh, she thought to herself, interesting.

The fox was good at work. Office life was just as she thought it would be. She had no complaints whatsoever with the simple tasks she was required to perform, which included making photocopies and tea. As always, Kuzuha could easily spot shortcuts and made few wasted movements. She could set cantankerous office machines right in no time, and her boss complimented her on her tea-making abilities. She also had a forte for spotting mistakes in documents written by her male colleagues. It was such a profoundly unexceptional sort of place that there wasn't any competition between female employees over impressing the high-earning male staff, and Kuzuha's excellence didn't seem to bother them. Her competence was hurled into her bosses' mouths along with their afternoon sweets, washed down with their tea, then promptly forgotten about.

Around the same time that the Glico-Morinaga scandal was making headlines, the Equal Employment Opportunity Law came into force. Ostensibly, the law set out to "secure equality of opportunity and treatment between men and women within the field of employment," but in reality, it was a bunch of empty promises. A few of the female employees complained about it in the staff kitchen or the locker rooms, but Kuzuha only thought, Well, there you have it. After all, she was a girl. For some reason, Kuzuha found the sound of the word *girl* most pleasant. Yep, she liked to say to herself, I'm a girl. I'm just a girl, after all.

When she saw men struggling with their work, Kuzuha would sometimes be overcome by pity, and would long to step in to help them. I could do that in a flash, Kuzuha would think. How unfair society was! Male employees had to pretend to be capable of doing things they couldn't do, while female employees had to pretend to be incapable of doing things they actually could do. Over the years, how many women had seen their talents magically disappear in that way? How many men had seen talents they didn't possess magically summoned into existence? Kuzuha let such thoughts float through her mind. Then she figured that this stuff didn't really have anything to do with her, and she promptly forgot all about it.

One winter's night in a lonely corner of the office, when most of the other employees had gone home, Kuzuha brought a cup of tea to Mr. Abe, the company's least competent worker, who was always getting in trouble for some mistake he'd made. His paper-strewn desk was a total shambles, and his suit was riddled with creases. Why does this man have to strive like this when he's so clearly incapable? Kuzuha wondered. I could've done this in five minutes.

"Looks like you're having a hard time of it, Mr. Abe," she said with genuine sympathy. He really was a poor soul.

Abe looked down at the cup of white, cloudy liquid that Kuzuha placed on his desk, and an expression of astonishment spread across his simple, benign face.

"W-what is this?"

"It's kuzu-yu. Ground arrowroot and hot water. It'll warm your body."

A plume of steam floated up between the two of them.

After marrying Mr. Abe in her mid-twenties, Kuzuha left the company and not long afterward gave birth to a baby boy. She did not veer off the shortcut that she had chosen for herself.

Mr. Abe may have been hopeless at his job, but as a permanent employee of the company he had a stable salary, and, above all, he was a kindhearted man. Kuzuha found it touching to see him trying so desperately to appear manly, doing all he could to conceal from her his exhaustion and his frustration. Poor soul! Kuzuha, for her part, always did her best to reward her husband for his hard work, and as a couple they got on well. Getting on well with one's husband was a part of the shortcut she had mapped out, so it came extremely naturally to her.

Kuzuha had no complaints with her new life. She found the child-rearing, the housework, and other matters of home economics a piece of cake. In no time at all, her son was in high school and Kuzuha's workload dropped off substantially. Both her husband and her son were truly good sorts. Good genes, Kuzuha figured. They were considerate, and on Mother's Day each year, they would present her with a bouquet of red carnations. Huh, Kuzuha would think to herself every year, interesting.

Throughout her life, Kuzuha had always had the feeling that she was just pretending to be a regular woman. Of course, that was the path she had selected as a shortcut, and she had never once doubted that her decision had been the right one. But one day as she studied her aging face in the mirror, a face whose eyes seemed more vulpine than ever, a face that the years had made even narrower, it occurred to Kuzuha that maybe she really was a fox—a fox who had totally forgotten that she had transformed into a person at some point along the line. No sooner had the thought formulated itself than Kuzuha realized how ridiculous it was. She put it out of her mind and set about wiping the dust off the mirror with a tissue.

When Kuzuha's son moved out to attend university, Kuzuha found herself with even more time on her hands. She tried attending tanka-composition classes at the local community center, but they didn't do very much for her. Reading about the ecstasies and tragedies of love, and the various resentments that people of bygone days had felt, immortalized in the form of tanka, the only thought that crossed Kuzuha's mind was *Huh*. It wasn't as if people's emotions ever really evolved, for better or for worse. There were no particular feelings stashed away inside Kuzuha for which she was desperately seeking an outlet.

It's time to escape.

Kuzuha began to hear a voice.

It's time to get out, the voice would say, and then fall silent.

Escape what, though? Kuzuha didn't really get it. She was perfectly content with her life as it was.

In her fifties, Kuzuha developed a passion for mountain climbing. A neighbor invited her to climb Mount Takao, and Kuzuha accepted. Why not? she thought, and in no time at all, she was hooked. It was more or less the first hobby Kuzuha had ever had. She breathed the fresh air into her lungs, felt the pulse of the mountains with her whole body. *I bloody love the mountains!* she wanted to scream at the top of her lungs, but as a demure Japanese woman, of course she didn't. Everybody praised the formidable power she had in her legs. It was as if she'd been born to climb, a few people suggested, and Kuzuha thought that maybe they were right. Why hadn't she encountered mountain climbing earlier on in life? It seemed like a bit of a shame.

At first, Kuzuha climbed as part of a group, but no one else could keep up with the pace she set, so at some point she began climbing alone. She'd load rice balls and slices of rolled omelette into her rucksack, fill her flask with tea, tie tight the shoelaces of her chunky climbing shoes, and head determinedly into the mountains.

The mountains always welcomed her. She liked the feeling of post-climb fatigue, too. It was the first tiredness she'd felt in her life. Who would ever have thought it was so pleasurable? Impressed, Kuzuha vowed to remember this lesson life had taught her.

When Kuzuha was in the mountains, the shortcuts disappeared from her head. She understood that mountains were dangerous places, so she was not permitted to stray off course—she had learned as much during her initiation phase. And yet, as she grew more experienced, she began to cave to the pull of temptation, to deviate from the path. Gradually, just a little at a time, and always so that she'd be able to find her way back, Kuzuha veered off the beaten track.

One day, after forcing her way into a forest adjoining the path, Kuzuha stepped off the edge of a cliff.

The branch she tried to grab on to slipped from her fingers, and she found herself free-falling through the air.

I'm going to die, Kuzuha thought to herself. Well, never mind. It was a good life I had.

She screwed her eyes shut.

The next instant, her body curled into a perfect ball and executed fifteen perfect 360-degree rotations, landing at the bottom of the cliff on all fours. *Well!* Kuzuha looked down at her slender front legs covered in white fur. Swiveling her head back, she saw a body, also covered in white fur, complete with a fuzzy tail. When she squinted, she could see a damp little nose just under her eyes, twitching. So, I really was a fox all along. Suddenly a lot of things made sense to Kuzuha. No wonder she'd been so good at being a Japanese woman!

Kuzuha let out a long howl, which went echoing out along the foot of the cliff. Damn, that felt good! And she could hear better, too. Before, the rustling of the trees had been just a far-off presence, a mere block of sound, but now she could make out the cadence of each individual leaf blowing against the wind. Neat, Kuzuha thought to herself.

Kuzuha the beautiful white fox began to run. Like a tightly wound spring suddenly released, the power in her body unfurled itself and Kuzuha went shooting through the green-shrouded forest. The soil she kicked up flew out on either side of her, adding to her momentum.

Gosh, thought Kuzuha as she darted forward, how tedious human life was! The way she'd become used to continually paring down her strength—all that time, she'd been betraying herself! Being unable to fully exert herself had been unbearably dull. Oh, what a stupid situation to have landed myself in! Kuzuha found it all so ridiculous. Feeling a pang of hunger, she ripped off a few wild grapes from their tangled vines, chomping them with great gnashes of her jaw. Purple juice dribbled down the sides of her crimson mouth, but that didn't bother her. Then Kuzuha's glinting eyes fell on a field mouse. The last thing the ill-fated creature saw was the film of saliva spreading across the red insides of the white fox's mouth.

Then Kuzuha ran up the cliff she'd fallen off. When she reached the top, she spun around once and, hey presto, she was a person again. How very convenient! Kuzuha smiled, retied her shoelaces, and trotted home on her human limbs.

•

"If you were an animal, you'd definitely be a fox," the young man next to Kuzuha had piped up out of the blue.

Kuzuha's eyes twinkled. "*If,* you say . . ."

When he'd first joined the company earlier that year, the young man had worn a permanently glum expression and was forever gazing down at his shoes. The other people in the company referred to him as "that depressed-looking boy" and "the miserable kid." Recently, though, he'd started to lighten up a bit. Even this ridiculously bad conversation opener was kind of cute, Kuzuha thought. At any rate, it was a hundred times better than that creepy old guy who'd told her at their first meeting that she looked like a fox before placing his hand on her knee. What a horrible, senseless age it had been, Kuzuha thought, when that kind of sexual harassment was so rife that nobody batted an eyelid when it happened.

After he'd got used to life in the company, the young man was moved over from the production line to Kuzuha's section. He certainly didn't look like he was harboring any special abilities, but Mr. Tei must have had some kind of plan in mind for him. Kuzuha was told to show him around and give him a feel for the kind of tasks their work involved.

For the first time in her life, Kuzuha was doing a job where she felt she was putting her talents to good use. In fact, until now, she'd thought that phrase—*putting your talents to good use*—was just some sinister nonsense they spouted in ads, but she'd discovered that it really was a concrete, material thing that mattered. Doing a job where you could put your talents to good use, where it was okay to go at things with everything you had, was wonderful. Having hidden her power away for so long, Kuzuha had a whole load saved up.

Kuzuha couldn't help but feel sympathy for this young man walking beside her now, in the process of shedding his melancholy. The poor guy, she thought. What had he done to deserve being flung out into such a world?

Society had changed a great deal since Kuzuha's time working in an office. She'd heard that now it was hard even for men to become fully fledged employees with permanent contracts. Society had become more equal, but in a bad way. Women hadn't risen up—rather the men had slid down. Kuzuha knew that the glass ceiling, which had previously been apparent only to women, was now visible to this young man, too.

I bet that comes as a surprise to you, doesn't it?

Kuzuha wanted to say to him. *It's different from how you were told it would be, right? You know what, though? As women, we've grown up with that ceiling since we were tiny. There was never a time when we couldn't see it. But somehow or other, we've all managed to live with it. It'll work out in the end for you, too.*

Kuzuha wanted to tell this young man all that, but she guessed he'd figure it out for himself eventually. That didn't stop her feeling sympathetic toward him, though, especially when she considered that not only did he have the ceiling to contend with—he also had to endure being watched over by men of the older generation, and being told to bear all the pressures that came with being a man. *Just take it, go on! Take it like we've done all this time!* Kuzuha figured that must be tough. At the end of the day, he'd just have to learn to ignore those older guys. Times changed, after all. Having observed them quietly throughout her life, Kuzuha could say with confidence that most of those men were basically scum.

In one way, the quantity of despair that men and women were feeling would soon become more or less equal. Maybe that would make it an easier world for people to live in, Kuzuha caught herself thinking somewhat indifferently, as if it was unrelated to her.

And indeed, it was unrelated to her. Such things were affairs for people, not foxes.

Standing in front of the door to her office, Kuzuha, the department head, opened the door for the young man beside her.

What She Can Do

From where they stood, it was all her fault. She was
entirely to blame.

She'd left home, taking the child with her and
bringing her short-lived marriage to an end. In more
ways than one, her other half wasn't the paternal sort,
the husbandly sort. In more ways than one, he wasn't
the child-support-paying sort either.

It was her fault, they thought, for not considering
her child. For getting divorced, for becoming a single mother. She was in the wrong because she hadn't
properly thought through the consequences. She was
wrong for prioritizing her own needs.

What was she supposed to do now? She felt utterly lost. She had no one to turn to. She needed to work and she needed to look after her young child, but there was only one of her. She was so desperate that she'd gladly have accepted help from a cat, but even if a cat had consented to step to her aid, there wasn't much it could have done.

There was no one around to tell her about the benefits she was entitled to. They looked coldly on her situation. She had brought it on herself, they said, and refused to proffer a helping hand. This would be a test of her capabilities, they declared, resolving to watch how much she could accomplish on her own, eagerly anticipating the moment when they would be able to point, their chests puffed out in self-satisfaction, and say, "See! I told you so!" They didn't feel any twinge of pain or guilt about adopting such an attitude. It was her own fault, after all.

"Still, you have to feel sorry for that poor child." They frowned and nodded with knowing expressions as their mouths formed these words of truth.

"A parent's selfishness hurts the child the most."

"The child is always the greatest victim in these situations."

"Bringing such misfortune on her own child! What a cruel-hearted woman she must be!"

She goes to work. So that she and the child can get by, she works morning and night. Her mind and her body suffer, and still, she continues to work. They can hardly believe it. What is she thinking, working like that all the time and never spending any time with her child? Can such a person even be called a mother? No, let us be clear. A person like her does not deserve to be called a mother.

What's more, to go by what they've heard, her night job is an, ahem, *night job.* Well, there you have it! A perfect fit for a woman of such loose morals! It's all turning out just as we thought, they say, shaking their heads. They shake and shake, throwing their heads from side to side with such force it's a miracle they don't snap off. Everything is proceeding just as they imagined. It's always the same with women like her—they all make the same mistakes. So dumbfounded are they by her flagrant lack of morals that they look to their own lives, their own lifestyles, and are relieved to discover how upright they appear in comparison, how little resemblance there is between them and her.

They don't know this (and if they did they'd most

certainly fall into a spluttering fit), but when she goes out to her night job, she takes the risk of leaving her daughter alone in the house. She doesn't have parents or friends who can look after the child, and she cannot afford to pay for a regular babysitter.

Please let her behave today. Please don't let anything happen to her.

Every day when she goes out to work she has to pray like this, as if she's gambling, as if she's writing a wish on one of those little slips of paper they hang up in the supermarket in July during the Tanabata festival. At work, all decked out in her slinky dress, speaking in a slinky voice, she can't shake off her anxiety. Life feels like a never-ending game of Russian roulette. Just because today was okay doesn't mean that tomorrow will be too. There is no end in sight. And yet she can't do anything about it. She has no way out.

So she decides to step in and help. She has been observing the tricky situation of the woman and child. That's part of her job.

First of all, she makes sure she has a thorough grasp of the issue. She then summarizes it in a report and submits it to her boss. Her boss passes eyes framed by thick black-rimmed spectacles over the report, immediately approves it, and sends her out on the case.

After the woman leaves for work, she quietly watches over the child. The room is somewhat messy. She decides to tidy up a little—not so much that it'll be obvious right away, but just a bit.

The child notices her there right from the start. At first, the child pretends to play on her own, but then she can't contain herself anymore and moves over to the corner, where she sits dead upright. Not easily intimidated, the child reaches out a hand to her kimono in amazement. She seems fascinated by the feel of it, so different to the clothes that she herself is wearing. Looking down with great tenderness at the child stroking her kimono, she produces a sweet from the fold of her wide sleeve and hands it to the child. The child gladly takes the sweet and begins sucking it. Each time the sweet moves in the child's mouth, a lump appears in one of her cheeks. Seeing this, she smiles in satisfaction.

Sweets are her secret weapon. With sweets, she always manages to win children over. For a long time, she used to pay daily visits to the sweetshop, but at some point she realized it was an ineffective way of going about things, and instead started to carry a stockpile around with her. The owner of the sweet-shop seems pleased by her decision to visit more infrequently too, although she could never understand why he found her presence quite so terrifying. Now she pops one into her own mouth, and looks at the child, mirroring the child's one-cheeked lump. Soon they are old friends. After all, in the past she had gone by the name of the Child-Rearing Ghost. That wasn't a title they gave you for nothing. There were very few children who didn't take to her. "Hey, ghost lady!" they would call out to her affectionately.

As soon as she began babysitting, she felt absolutely certain that this was what she'd been born (and had died) to do. (It should be acknowledged that she was headhunted for the position. Someone must have noticed her suitability for the work before she did.) While alive, it never once occurred to her that she'd find a job so perfect for her in the afterlife. In fact, she had never worked in her life. But jobs aren't at all bad—that's her view on the matter now.

When the child falls asleep, exhausted from all her playing, she gives the room a cursory cleanup and waits for the mother to come home. She looks around the room she shares with the child. She sees boxes crammed with stuffed toys and picture books, walls plastered with crayon drawings the child has made, a somewhat dingy balcony where clothes have been hung out to dry.

She'd like to show them this place. She thinks the same of all of the homes she visits. Here is a place where two people go about their lives. A place where two people are living, striving to keep going. What right do they have to bad-mouth her when they've never even stepped foot inside her life? They should save it for when they've seen it from the inside. Then they can bad-mouth all they want. Honestly, who do they think they are, pretending to be so clever when they lack the skills to come in, look around, walk about? They should all just die—and then come back again. She can't understand them at all.

She's done all there is to do and is sitting very still watching the baby's sleeping face as the woman comes home. She kicks off her shoes at the door and rushes straight to the back room where the child is sleeping.

The woman doesn't notice her sitting there. But she doesn't go out of her way to make her presence known. There is no need to rush things. As the days go by, she will come to notice her gradually. She will come to sense her presence in the emotional stability of her child, in the tidiness of her apartment, and then she will be ready to accept her. When that happens, she can proceed to the next level, and make herself seen. She will be able to openly help her in all aspects of her life. She will be freed from the game of Russian roulette, and at some point, a friendship will begin to blossom between the two. It has always been that way in the past.

She can make her and the child happy. That's the thing she feels the most proud of. It's something they can't do, something they don't even attempt to do. But she can do it, and she will do it. That's what sets her apart from them. She is relieved by how little resemblance there is between her and them. She watches her as she squeezes the child's hand and lets out a big sigh, and she nods in satisfaction.

She touches her hand very gently to the child's cheek, and then starts to change out of her work clothes. The slinky dress falls to the floor in a puddle, so she appears to be standing in a pool of still water. Her day's work is over.

As one of them vanishes, the other takes a shower, burrows her squeaky-clean face next to the child, and falls asleep.

Enoki

At first, Enoki was utterly confused.

It started suddenly. Without any forewarning or explanation, people began visiting. They came in droves to find her. Initially, Enoki had no idea what they had come for. When she finally understood, she was flabbergasted.

Yes, she was aware that there was something a little unusual about her body. Specifically, she had two largish burrs on the lower section of her trunk. But she thought nothing of it. Everything and everyone has an idiosyncrasy or two, including hackberries like herself. It's hardly anything to marvel at. Nowadays, people term it "individuality." In any case, the lumps were no big deal to Enoki, and she didn't give them much thought. Burrs were just burrs.

And yet, people said that Enoki was special. People took her knobbly, rounded outgrowths for something extraordinary. They stood in front of them and prayed, and carried off the resin oozing out of them. What on earth was going on? Their behavior bewildered Enoki. It seemed to her a kind of madness.

The women were particularly strange. Watching all these desperate women as they joined their hands in prayer and bowed their heads to her, Enoki felt she was missing something. It was something she never truly got used to, but in the beginning, when she was particularly unused to it, she would feel the rage bubbling up inside her. What the hell are you people playing at?

When it first occurred to Enoki that people saw her burrs as breasts and her resin as milk, she shuddered. Even now, when she recollects that day, there is only one word to describe her feeling, and that word is *disgust*.

Allegedly, the "sweet dew" that was Enoki's resin had special properties. If mothers with trouble lactating rubbed the resin on their breasts, they would start producing milk. Give me a break!

Allegedly, Enoki's "sweet dew" was no different from human breast milk, so if the rubbing proved fruitless, you could feed the resin directly to your babies and they would grow up healthy and strong. Give me a break, guys!

Every time she heard people around her in the shrine grounds spouting this crazy nonsense, Enoki would shout the same thing in her mind, flapping her leaves in frantic resistance, but nobody noticed. Everyone was so obsessed by her burrs and her resin, they had no time for anything else.

People loved to see things in other things. Enoki knew that very well. You could even say that this was the starting point for all religion, and moreover, that it wasn't always a bad thing. But when people saw the burrs on her body as human breasts, Enoki felt a strong discomfort. Her burrs were just plain old burrs, and her resin definitely wasn't "sweet dew." In fact, she sometimes found herself worrying about the adverse effect it might have on the human body if ingested. Surely you really shouldn't be feeding young human bodies that stuff? But the humans were just that eager to depend upon Enoki's special powers—powers that Enoki herself didn't believe in.

After years mulling over her inexplicable disgust,

Enoki concluded that what she truly objected to was the way in which humans used their own yardsticks to affix meanings onto things that had nothing to do with them. They did this to objects around them, and even to elements of nature. People would pick vegetables that looked like parts of the human body, then feature them in TV news items about how "obscene" they were, when really the only thing making those vegetables "obscene" was the gaze of the people looking at them. A firm udon noodle was, for some reason, compared to the tautness of the female body; varieties of fruits were assigned women's names. When she put together all the information she'd accumulated over time, Enoki had no choice but to conclude that human beings derived joy from twisting things and attaching a sexual meaning to them. It was pathetic. Were they idiots? Was that it? And then to cap it all, they turned to Enoki, who wasn't even a mother, and their mouths formed the words *breast milk*. Enoki hated the very sound of it: *breast milk*. There was a precariousness to it. It could ruin you if you weren't careful. She couldn't explain it, but Enoki knew that instinctively. She hated that she'd been dragged into all of this—that *parts* of her had been dragged into all of this.

And yet, the sadness those women felt—that was

different. That was real. Enoki can still vividly recall the faces of all the women who came to visit her. She feels awful for women who lived back then, before formula milk existed. Of course, nowadays, with the humans' deep-rooted devotion to the religion of breastfeeding, women still suffer a lot, but the invention of formula must have improved things. There's a sizeable difference between having something to serve as a replacement, and having no such thing. Options are crucial, and women suffered in the past because they had none.

Speaking of which . . . Once upon a time there was a woman called Okise. She was raped by a man who threatened to kill her baby if she refused to have sex with him. He continued to rape her, then killed her husband and assumed his place as her new spouse.

That's barbaric enough as it is, but it gets worse, because from that point on, Okise stopped producing breast milk. Her new husband suggested that if she couldn't produce milk of her own, she ought to give her baby away. Unable to nourish her own child, Okise had no choice but to hand over her beloved boy to someone else. If only there had been formula milk back in those days!

"It's okay. I can just use formula," Okise would have

replied coolly, clasping her son close. The husband, realizing how unfeasible his suggestion was, would have dropped the subject.

Anyway, it turned out that the old man to whom the baby was entrusted had been instructed by the husband to kill it. Fortunately, though, he was won over by the adorable baby, and decided to raise the child in secret.

Funnily enough, the thing the old man struggled most with was securing breast milk for the baby. As an old man, there were no strings he could pull in that regard, so he had little choice but to rely on the goodwill of various women he met. After just about scraping by that way for a while, the old man caught wind of a rumor, and not long after, he appeared in front of Enoki. That was how Enoki came to know of Okise. The baby drank the "milk" coming out of Enoki's "breasts" and grew up to be healthy and strong. Of course, this only consolidated the myth of Enoki's magic, and so she became a bona fide legend. Yet Enoki still finds the whole thing very suspicious. It was just too outlandish to believe. The old man must have been feeding the baby something else as well. In any case, Enoki wants to believe that he was, because she definitely doesn't have such powers.

Okise, on the other hand, subsequently gave birth to the child of her new husband, but because she couldn't produce milk, the baby died. Not long after, a mysterious growth appeared on Okise's breasts, and she went crazy and died too. Why is it that a woman who was repeatedly raped, then had her child stolen away from her, had to meet with such a cruel fate? Why did a series of such awful things have to befall her breasts? Well, gods? Don't you think that's overkill?

And the tale of Okise was just one example. The pain and the sadness that women felt when it came to breast milk reached depths Enoki could not fathom. Enoki's sticky old resin was the last ray of hope for those women. So they clung to her. Through her thick bark, she sensed the enormous determination coming off their bodies. She felt, too, the tenderness and the strength of their breasts. How different they were from Enoki's hard, knobbly ones. She felt like it was an insult to these women to call her organs by the same name. Enoki couldn't bear it. These women were doing all they could to be saved by her nonexistent supernatural powers, and she couldn't do a thing for them. She knew that it was hardly her fault, but still she found it tough.

•

These days, hardly anyone comes to visit Enoki. She's become nothing but an old relic. On rare occasions, some strange type with a fixation for legends of the past will take the trip out to see her. "Ah, it must be that one," she'll hear someone say. They look at her as if she's a museum exhibit and take photos. Women at their wits' end no longer come to see Enoki. She's sure they must still exist, but in any case, they have no need to rely on her anymore.

Enoki has never for a second believed that she has the special powers that everyone thinks she has, but just hypothetically speaking, if she had, then she would have served a function not dissimilar to that of formula milk in the days before it existed. With this in mind, she feels she can finally accept the crazy commotion that descended on her back then.

The shrine grounds are quiet. Enoki can hear a bird somewhere off in the distance. The wind ruffles her leaves indifferently. Now nothing, nobody, pays Enoki any attention. The days pass. The seasons change. Enoki isn't lonely. If anything, she is relieved. The pressure on her has finally lifted. As it has always been, really, her resin is now just resin, and her burrs are just burrs.

At last, Enoki can be just a tree.

Silently Burning

It always makes me nervous when they stare at my hands. Taking care not to falter, I set my brush down on the open page of the album I've been entrusted with and begin to write. Whatever happens, I mustn't make a mistake. Meanwhile, the owner of the album stands on the other side of the counter of the small temple office, staring fixedly at my handiwork. Maybe she isn't actually staring, but I feel like she is.

The visitor is a woman in her fifties. She's most likely concerned because I appear too young to be doing this job. I'm not wearing any makeup, and with my jet-black hair in a simple shoulder-length cut, I probably look even younger than I am. I have bangs, which doesn't help matters either. As more people hand over their albums to me, their hesitation is palpable. "Is the chief priest not in today?" some of them ask, their eyes full of misgivings. Their fervent hope that it'll be the chief priest who writes in their album rather than me spills out of their every pore.

All this makes me a bit despondent, but I can understand why they would feel that way. The younger someone is, the less accomplished their calligraphy is likely to be—that's the simple fact of the matter. People treasure their shuin albums, and if they've gone out of their way to get them signed and stamped, then they want them to look as elegant as possible. They want the calligraphy to be beautiful. I don't have an album but if I did, I'm sure I'd feel the same. Ultimately, though, everyone gets it: album-signing is about the unpredictable, unrepeatable encounter between calligrapher and album owner. That's all part of the fun.

When I've finished, I cover my handiwork with a piece of thin blotting paper cut to exactly the right size, then close the album. With the blotting paper on top I can still see the letters I have inked, but it looks as if the text has moved farther away, something I always find a bit disconcerting. Cutting pieces of blotting paper in half so that they fit the albums is one of several tasks I perform when I have nothing else to do. There is always a good number of people visiting the temple to collect stamps, so if I don't cut up fresh batches of blotting paper regularly, I often end up short.

"That's three hundred yen," I say, returning the album with its prettily patterned washi cover to its owner. The woman must have had her money ready because it appears on my palm instantly, like some magic trick. Under the overcast, drizzling sky, the three silver coins are dazzlingly bright.

I assume the woman must have checked my handiwork then and there, because as I am putting the money away, I hear her speak.

"But what lovely writing!" Her words seem to have flown out of her mouth of their own accord.

"Thank you," I say, looking up and then immediately dipping my head. I'm not very good at looking people in the eye while I talk.

There is a particular expression that most people's faces take on when they see my calligraphy, somewhere between surprise and satisfaction. Their expressions also say, *I'm glad I got this girl to write in my album.* It seems like the more they doubt my abilities to begin with, the more overjoyed they are when they see the results. It's hardly my fault if they decide to underestimate what a young woman like me is capable of, but I'm still relieved to see them looking pleased.

I've been studying calligraphy since I was small. The other kids I knew all turned their noses up at it because it was uncool, but I liked the hush that would settle within me when I was doing it. The simplicity of the world that took shape on the page in front of me, a world made up of ink, and ink alone, provided me with an escape route from the blaring clatter of the outside world.

While I was at university, the chief priest at my local temple began to suffer from chronic back pain, and a neighbor introduced me as a potential replacement. That was how I came by my first temporary job as temple calligrapher. Strictly speaking, it wasn't just calligraphy I was doing—there were other menial tasks involved, but I enjoyed those, too. There was something deeply satisfying about having a fixed, unchanging set of duties to accomplish.

Even after graduating from university I continued to attend calligraphy lessons, and so the job offers kept coming. Sometimes I'd go to different temples on different days of the week, but my tasks were always pretty much the same. Every day, I would sit there, brush in hand, and write.

I found I liked sitting in the spot reserved for the calligrapher inside the temple office, which sold talismans and ema—wooden plaques for people to write their prayers on. All kinds of people would come by, do whatever they'd come to do, and leave. There were always certain locals who came day in, day out, and whom I got to know by sight. Sometimes they would give me boiled sweets or little cakes. Perhaps they found it funny, seeing a young person like me sitting there so solemnly in my monk's work clothes. I've always been told that I don't have a very expressive face.

People come to temples to pray for different things: safety for their family, academic success, safety on the roads, warding off evil, luck in love, and so on. They pray, and I watch. I come to the temple practically every day, but I've never once prayed. I guess it's not just expressiveness I'm lacking in, but feelings, too—by which I mean to say, I don't have any idea what I'd pray for. I don't have any wishes. Even when I was little, and all the other kids would write their wishes on colored strips of paper to be strung up for the Tanabata festival, I would never have anything to write. But I liked the act of writing on those little slips so much, I'd invent wishes just so I could write them all down, filling in strips on my friends' behalf too.

Even romantic relationships hold little interest for me. They come and they go, without my ever feeling any real sense of involvement.

Anyway, as I worked between different temples I realized that I had become a kind of traveling calligrapher. Every time I visited a new temple and showed the chief priest and his wife a sample of my calligraphy, they would look both pleased and relieved, and comment that they could see they were in safe hands with me. Whatever kind of day it was—sunny, or rainy, or white with snow—the world seen from the temple office always looked a little distant, and tranquil, as if I were standing on the edge of the world looking in.

"What are these netsuke supposed to be?" A woman whose album I'd just signed addresses me. I'd assumed our interaction was over when I saw her tuck away the finished album inside her LeSportsac bag, so I'd tuned out. Now I have no idea what she's talking about and feel flustered. I am rarely asked questions, and it takes me a while to gear up to answer them.

I follow the direction of the woman's gaze and see that she is looking at the metal netsuke, arranged next to the talismans to ward off fire. The netsuke are little oblong ornaments with tiny bells attached to them, and the sections intended to signify empty spaces have been filled in with patterns, so I can see how they might be hard to identify. They look a bit like miniature slatted fences.

"Oh, those . . . They're . . . They're ladders."

The woman's face resolves itself into a look of comprehension.

"Oh, of course! This is the Oshichi temple, isn't it?"

"Yes, that's right."

The woman nods, then briskly walks away.

Visitors to this temple fall roughly into three categories:

1. people who happen to be passing and decide to drop in;
2. people who come with a purpose—maybe because they're collecting temple stamps, or they want to

pray—but aren't really aware what
kind of temple this is;

3. people who come here because of
    Oshichi, the greengrocer's daughter.

You can subdivide this last category into two further categories: a) those who aren't in love with anyone at the moment but feel a connection with Oshichi
and want to pay her a visit; and b) those who have a
special someone in mind and come to pray to Oshichi
for luck in love.

I've been working at this temple for a few years
now, and in this regard, it's a little different from
all the others. Visitors to other temples fall exclu-
sively into categories 1 and 2, but because this temple
has Oshichi's grave inside its grounds, it boasts this
unique third category of attendees.

I wasn't aware of this until I started working here,
but it is believed that Oshichi was an actual person,
burned at the stake a few hundred years ago for arson.
Allegedly, it was rare for women to be dealt that pun-
ishment at that time, but somehow Oshichi managed
it. What was more, her reason for committing arson
was none other than love. So badly had she yearned
to see her beloved again, she'd set her house on fire so

she could take refuge in the temple where he worked. Her story captured people's imaginations, and has been retold goodness knows how many times since. Some accounts claim she didn't actually set anything on fire, that she had merely climbed up the ladder in the village and sounded the bell and beat the drum and done all the other things that were done back in the day to alert the villagers to a fire, thereby creating an excuse to see her love. She was an old-school romantic type, you could say, definitely on the obsessive end of the spectrum. So, it follows that people who fall into the third category—those who deliberately come here to pray for luck in love at Oshichi's temple—often seem to be of that same type. I can identify them immediately. All 3s—for some reason the 3s are almost always women—tend to behave exactly the same way.

A 3 enters the temple grounds with a determined stride and heads straight to Oshichi's grave. Like Oshichi, her unerring gaze is fixed on one thing alone, and she registers interest in nothing else. Her prayers are protracted. Her offerings are more generous than those of other visitors. She places flowers on Oshichi's grave or presents her with other gifts she has brought. Then she stands there for a curiously long time. Possibly she is talking to Oshichi inside her head, telling her the things that she can't tell other people. On occasion, the length of time that a 3 spends in front of the grave will beggar belief.

When the 3 finally tears herself away from Oshichi, she proceeds to the main temple, where once again she spends a long time in prayer. She doesn't scrimp on her offering there, either. Then she drops by the temple office, where I am sitting, and wordlessly buys up ladder netsuke and various talismans, as if she has researched them all beforehand and knows exactly what they signify. At this time, she reminds me of a die-hard fan stocking up on merchandise. Finally, the 3 calls in one more time at Oshichi's grave, offers another protracted prayer, and then leaves the temple with the same determined stride that marked her entrance.

Watching this sequence from the temple office, I am awed. I don't have an obsessive personality, but these women remind me a lot of certain friends of mine who are fixated on something—figure skating, a particular pop star, a hobby, what have you. Somewhere inside, these people are all quietly on fire. I get the feeling that Japanese women have a peculiar capacity for obsession. When they are truly into something, they are absolutely single-minded in their fixation. They give it all they have. They throw heaps of money at it, research it endlessly, and do whatever seems necessary to draw closer to it. You sense real passion there.

Imagine if someone like that fell for, say, a work colleague, with the same passion. As a full-grown adult, she can hardly let those roaring flames in her chest govern her behavior, and so some of her passion is left unspent. Maybe that's why such women visit Oshichi's grave. They want to pay their respects to the woman who allowed the flames of her passion to blaze to their fullest, and who was herself burned at the stake as a result. Most likely they feel like Oshichi is the only one who can understand the fire inside them. The very idea that you have to rein in your heat even as love's passion sets you ablaze . . . How restrictive life as a functional adult is!

When I first started working at the Oshichi temple, the idea of praying for luck in love to someone who'd been burned at the stake for her excess of passion seemed like a sick joke, but as I watched the 3s visit, I started to understand their motivation a lot better. By coming here, these women feel themselves connected with Oshichi across time. I started to think myself lucky to be working at such a temple, where all the Oshichi types congregate.

•

Seeing now that the temple grounds are empty, I step out of the office and quickly stroll around to check that everything is in order, then move over to Oshichi's grave and sweep away the leaves that have gathered there. The fine drizzle has stopped, but the sky is still clouded over. Then, noticing an elderly man on the narrow path leading up to the temple, I slip back inside the office inconspicuously.

As I settle down on my floor cushion, I realize I've left the radio on. It's an old bright red model that the priest has let me use so long as nobody is around. The voice coming from the speakers says something about a skeleton that has gone missing from some research institute. *The police are currently investigating the identity of a mystery woman discovered on the security camera footage.* The news item comes to an end, and I turn the radio off.

A *skeleton*? I cock my head in disbelief as I quickly wipe down my desk. The phrase "mystery woman" makes me picture a long-haired figure in a trench coat and sunglasses, but what did she really look like? I wonder. What could she have wanted badly enough with a skeleton that she would steal it from a research institute? A peculiar news item, no mistake. Still, peculiar things happen from time to time.

The old man appears outside the office, so I slide open the glass window and he holds out his album. I can see that slightly anxious expression on his face, which means, *Surely it's not this girl who's going to do it?*

"Just a moment, please," I say quietly. I ink up the stamps and press them onto the page, then take out my brush. The man moves two or three steps back and waits, fidgeting. I write the date in the corner followed by the usual characters, then place a square of blotting paper on top.

"Here you are," I hesitantly call to the gray-haired man, who has now moved a little way off, and return his album. He hands me his three hundred yen, nods in thanks, and moves off. As he walks away, I see him open it up to check its newest entry, then turn back to glance at me, a look of astonishment on his face.

With nothing in particular to do, I decide to take stock of the office supplies. Noticing that we are down to the very last surplus page—the pages we pre-prepare for people who have come without their albums, so they can stick them in at a later date—I set about creating some more.

As I am writing away on those bits of paper, the priest's wife pops in to see how I am getting on.

"Someone brought these around for us earlier." She places a little paper-wrapped cake on the corner of my desk together with a cup of green tea, then stands there watching me, a satisfied expression on her face. "You know, there's something about the way you write. It's not just proficient—there's something a little fierce, a little passionate about it. Fiery, I suppose you could say. It just goes to show that you really can't judge a book by its cover."

This isn't the first time the priest's wife has paid me a compliment of this kind. Though I'm not too sure what they mean, both the chief priest and his wife seem to be under the impression that my calligraphy is a perfect match for Oshichi.

After the priest's wife leaves, I continue making the surplus pages. There are two other part-time workers at the temple, but they can't do calligraphy, so it seems like a good idea to get a bunch done while I have the chance.

At some point, I realize that dusk is falling. Even on a cloudy day like today, the setting sun is a proper vivid red. On the other side of the sliding window, I keep on moving my brush in silence.

A New Recruit

I made my way through the entrance hall to find a lobby with a sofa and a cloakroom that appeared unattended. To my left was a staircase leading up to the first floor, but instead I continued walking down the long corridor that stretched straight ahead. The carpet with its throng of woven flowers and birds was slightly faded, but I could tell that it must've once been magnificent. From behind a dark partition, I could hear the sounds of ongoing construction work. People who seemed to be hotel employees emerged from the large banquet room and disappeared behind another door. The whole place was rather dingy.

Just as I was thinking how all of this was rather different to what I had imagined, I came across the shopping arcade. Unfolding on either side of me was a row of small shops: exclusive boutiques catering to wealthy ladies; a shoeshine place with a stylish sign; a shop selling a famous brand of cosmetic blotting paper; and then, at the very end of the corridor, a reception desk for an outdoor pool.

As I drew closer to the glass wall, decorated with colorful pictures of palm trees and such, I could see a young woman in a bikini facing this way, addressing a staff member at the counter. His colleague next to him looked away, bored. Near the counter, opposite another pane of glass that separated the indoor pool from the outdoor one, a man in shorts and a short-sleeved linen shirt was watching their interaction. I guessed he must be the woman's father.

Perhaps sensing eyes on her, the girl turned around to look at me, then twisted her bare leg in discomfort. I found it rather funny that, though we were only separated by a sheet of glass, there she was in a bikini while I was in my suit. I averted my eyes. This year, as for many years now, I have had no contact whatsoever with swimming pools—or with the sea, for that matter.

At the very end of the passage was a door that appeared to lead through to the annex, but knowing that renovations were under way in that section of the building, I turned around without opening it. After retracing my steps, wondering what was going to become of all these stores as I did so, I found myself again at the entrance through which I'd come in.

I didn't understand. Could this really be the hotel whose planned refurbishment was causing such an outcry? Although I didn't dislike it in its existing form, from what I'd seen of it thus far there was nothing exceptional about it that needed to be preserved, and the decision to renovate it seemed totally reasonable. I couldn't see any sign of the section that everyone had been talking about.

At a loss, I walked over to the cloakroom and there, among the leaflets displayed in a row along the counter, I found one whose cover photograph showed the very spot I was looking for. I picked it up, then headed down the corridor again until I ran into an employee coming out of the banquet room.

"Excuse me. How do I get here?" I said, indicating the cover of the leaflet.

The man nodded and said, "Ah, that's the new wing you want. We're in the main building at the moment.

The lighting's very similar, so they're easily confused. You'll find the lobby for the new wing on the fourth floor."

"The fourth floor?" I said in surprise.

The man kindly showed me to the elevators before bowing and moving off. Seamlessly taking over from him, an elderly gentleman standing in front of the elevator smiled and opened the doors for me.

Inside the elevator, my eyes were drawn toward the large flowers woven across that small square of carpet, but I couldn't identify them. The feeling that I was trampling them made me somewhat uneasy, so I deliberately looked up. Was this how Tom Thumb had felt, I wondered, or the inch-high samurai?

The elevator reached the fourth floor in no time, and as I walked out through the open doors, to my right I saw the lobby whose pictures I'd seen several times online and in magazines. Just a glimpse was enough to understand why people would be mourning its disappearance.

On my way to the hotel, I'd walked past Toranomon Hospital and ascended the hill, then come in through the first entrance I'd seen, but I realized now that I'd used the entrance reserved for banquet guests. Had I only continued farther up the hill and come in through the main entrance, I'd have encountered this lobby right away.

By the entrance was a long reception counter behind which the desk staff and the concierge stood, and beside it was a rather stylish newspaper rack. To its side, behind a centrally positioned arrangement of large rocks and ikebana, was a luxuriously spacious salon. Around each of the round low tables, amply spaced out across the brown-and-beige-latticed carpet, a cluster of four or five armchairs were positioned like petals around a flower, entreating people to sit back and admire the view. Pretty lights strung together in rows were suspended from the ceiling and the walls were decorated with intricate patterns.

As I trod my path inside this gorgeous field of flowers, a woman on one of the sofas placed in the corners of the room—apparently a few of the petals had come loose and were floating free—looked up at me from her paperback. She was a petite woman with a softly sculpted bob. I made my way over in her direction, and her mouth, painted a pretty shade of coral, formed itself into a smile.

"You must be Mr. Tei," she said.

"Yes, that's right. I'm sorry to have kept you waiting."

The woman extended a milk-white palm to indicate the sofa opposite, and I sat down facing her. I presented her with my business card and introduced myself properly.

"I'm sorry to have brought you here on such a chaotic day," she said with a smile.

"Chaotic, you say?"

"Well, all these people who've come to say their last goodbyes."

Looking around me, I saw that there were indeed a fair number of people in the lobby, taking photos with their phones and digital cameras. A well-dressed woman with an expensive-looking SLR strode past us. It seemed that the hotel restaurant, which served lunch and afternoon tea, was about to open, and the elderly customers waiting to enter had begun piling up in the lobby. Everyone was dressed to the nines, speaking in animated tones.

"Such a waste!" the woman said softly, looking at them. "It's only been here fifty years . . ." Then she continued in a surprisingly matter-of-fact manner. "Still, I can't wait to see what the new building's going to be like! They're making it into a skyscraper, by all accounts. It's hard to imagine, isn't it? I wonder how it'll turn out."

She glanced up at the ceiling, as if she really was trying and failing to imagine what it would like. "I came here with my husband when it had just been built, you see. 'Showa Modern,' they called this style of architecture—a blend of the East and the West. It was the height of fashion back then, and we were ever so taken with it. We always came here on special occasions, when we wanted to splash out a bit, you know. Such wonderful memories."

As she spoke, her speech punctuated with little giggles, I nodded encouragingly. I sometimes felt envious of people like her, who'd lived in a time where the ultimate luxury was to get dressed up and dine out in a hotel for some special occasion, in a way that people of my generation would never think of doing. Back then, when they still had advertising balloons tethered to roofs, people would go shopping in department stores. They would eat omurice in the department store cafeterias, ride on the big observation wheels situated on the tops of the buildings. There were hardly any department stores with big wheels on their roofs now.

"That's why I came here, you see. I was in an old people's home for the last few years of my life, and during that time my children took over the house I'd been living in and had it renovated. I'm not resentful, mind. I've only good memories of this place, and with all the people coming and going, there's not been a dull moment."

"I totally understand."

I looked at the elegant woman sitting in front of me with her olive-green two-piece ensemble and her pearl necklace, her knees in their pearlescent stockings so neatly aligned. She'd have worn this when she came here with her husband, I thought. Deciding it was time to get down to business, I started, somewhat nervously:

"As I've mentioned before, we'd like to invite you to come to us while the main building is being renovated. Of course, I know that you could just move to the annex, but I thought it might be good for you to try out somewhere new. Have a change of scenery, you know. You could come back here once this place is renovated, or, of course, we'd be more than delighted for you to stay with us, if you decide to do so. We have women with all kinds of different talents at our company, and someone like you would be most welcome. You don't have to make a big commitment; you can just try it out and see what it's like. What do you think? Of course, I don't mean to pressure you."

I looked her straight in the eyes as I spoke. For

whatever reason, I've never been good at smiling on demand, not even in a professional context. All I could do was to speak as earnestly as possible.

"Yes, I suppose that's an idea." The woman brought her wrinkled white hand up to her wrinkled white cheek and a dreamy look came over her face. In this posture, she looked just like a little girl, although the middle finger of the hand resting on her cheek was adorned with a silver ring with a big glinting emerald. It made me think of the flyers for jewelry shops that one used to find inside newspapers along with all the other promotional leaflets. Now you rarely ever saw such flyers. When I'd first learned how to use scissors, I would cut out each and every one of the gems pictured in those leaflets, even the tiny, fussy ones. The rings with the spiky edges were my chance to show off my cutting skills. I refused to throw away the precious gemstones I'd cut out, storing them in an empty cookie tin instead. One time, I remembered, I'd presented my mom with a ruby ring that I'd cut out particularly well. She'd seemed genuinely pleased.

"Yes, maybe that would be best. In that case, perhaps I'll come to you when I've finished up here. That's okay, isn't it? I'd like to stay here until the very end, you see."

"Yes, by all means. That would be marvelous, thank you."

Before I knew what I was doing, I got to my feet and gave her a low, respectful bow.

"Oh, come now, don't be silly! I should be the one thanking you for agreeing to take on an old lady like me."

"Not at all, not at all."

She smiled slightly as if she found the whole interaction amusing, but I knew that she was simply unaware of the extent of her own powers. Having met so many of these kinds of women over the years, I'd come to realize that they consistently underestimate their abilities. Even with the knowledge of their full capabilities, they still fail to value themselves.

I sat down, scratching my head in slight embarrassment, and we chatted away for a while before she piped up. "Your Japanese is really excellent, Mr. Tei."

"Thank you," I said, glancing away. In doing so, I saw that the restaurant had now opened.

I was raised in Japan, so my Japanese isn't noticeably different from the average Japanese person's, and yet I'm often complimented on my Japanese—I suppose because of my name, which is noticeably un-Japanese-sounding, and my appearance. In my teens, this often left me feeling ostracized, but at some point it ceased to bother me. Nonetheless, it always struck me as very strange that even if you felt yourself the same as the person you were talking to, it didn't necessarily mean the other person saw you in that regard.

I offered to pick her up from the hotel the day it closed, but she assured me that she would manage to find us as long as she had a map, so I decided to take her word for it. I handed her a photocopy of the map showing the location of our company, then got to my feet and bowed once more, and she waved me goodbye. I inquired what her plans were for the rest of the day, and she told me that since it was getting a bit noisy down here, she would probably carry on reading her book at one of the desks upstairs. There was a little area with three wooden writing desks, she said, which had been her favorite spot for years now. The desks were separated from one another with partitions, each with its own lamp, and being there always put her in a special mood.

Walking toward the entrance, I realized how many more people there were now: asking the hotel staff to take their photos, strolling around, sitting and chatting in the comfortable chairs. I could only suppose they were all really going to miss this place, and now

I understood very well why that was. I could see that this hotel, this building, was the kind that induced those sorts of feelings in people.

When I turned to look back one last time, I caught sight of her amid all the hustle and bustle, making her way up the flight of stairs just as she'd said she would. From this angle, she looked exactly like a small child. Would this hotel get another zashiki warashi when she was gone? I prayed with all my heart that it would. Maybe she would even return here, when everything was complete. But in any case, while the renovations were taking place, I would be borrowing her.

One of my earliest memories is feeling a sense of incredulity at how many people there were in the world. As a small child, I was genuinely concerned that a world so swarming with people was liable to explode. It was a needless fear, though. Half the people I was seeing were no longer of this world.

I don't know why, but the living and the dead have always looked exactly the same to me. I spent my childhood in a state of profound confusion and then, as a teenager, I discovered the film *The Sixth Sense*. Aha! I remember thinking: This is me! (Obviously I don't mean Bruce Willis.) From that point on, I began to come to terms with my talent.

When you can see both the living and the dead, you realize that there is little difference. There are those with talent and those without it, among the living and the dead alike. They're really just the same. So I made the decision to assemble the talented ones from each—the best of both worlds, you could say.

I stepped out of the hotel and the big blue sky stretched overhead. Summer was coming to an end. Taxis pulled up in front of the hotel entrance in rapid succession. The word that popped to mind was *flocking*—surely there were few places so deserving of that word as this one. There weren't very many places people would flock to like this, just to offer their last goodbyes.

There was a spring in my step as I walked, perhaps because I was going downhill. Or perhaps I was in a upbeat mood due to my good scouting work: I figured that we'd be flooded with offers of temp work for her. Or, if she preferred to take up an internal position with us, we'd be only too pleased to oblige. In any case, I was heading straight back to the office, so I decided to take a little something with me to share out at the three o'clock snack break.

I paused in a shaded spot in the street and used the Tabelog app on my phone to check for a nice bakery or similar in the vicinity. I found a Japanese sweet-shop with a good reputation for mame daifuku, gooey dumplings stuffed with azuki bean paste—so I set Google Maps to direct me there. As I walked in the direction that the audio guide instructed, I pictured the fierce snatching match that would surely unfold over the mame daifuku and resolved to buy as many as I could.

Team Sarashina

Ms. Sarashina's team is really something else. No other team in our company comes even close to being as flexible as hers, though I must add that on the whole we are a pretty fluid organization when it comes to things like job description, work hours, and so on.

First off, the Sarashinas don't belong to any particular department. If you were forced to categorize them, they'd just be "The Sarashinas," or "Ms. Sarashina's Team," or something similar. In fact, the Sarashinas had no fixed location initially, but that began to discomfit Mr. Tei in view of their outstanding job performance. So, during the big shake-up that took place two years ago, he assigned them a small room of their own. I got the sense that this room had sort of sprung up out of nowhere between the admin office and Operation Room No. 5, but those kinds of things happen quite a lot at this company, so it wasn't surprising.

The Sarashinas were very bashful about the whole thing, and when Mr. Tei suggested having a nameplate made for their room, they chimed in collectively:

"Oh no!"

"No, no, please don't worry!"

"Honestly!"

"Don't trouble yourself."

"Please don't be silly!"

The nameplate suggestion was shelved, and for a while there was nothing at all outside the room. Just the other day, though, a piece of paper with the words TEAM SARASHINA written in red and black marker appeared on the wall outside their door. I figured they had finally adjusted to the idea of having their own room. Upon noticing it, Mr. Tei commented that they really must order a nameplate, but the Sarashinas once again refused:

"Oh no, really."

"No, no, please, drop the subject."

"We're honestly all right."

"This is fine, just as it is, really."

"Honestly, please."

The TEAM SARASHINA sign is decorated with maple leaves cut from red and orange paper. The leaves are somewhat uneven in shape and size in a way that suggests handicrafts are not Team Sarashina's strong suit, but they look pretty good nonetheless. I should add that even if handicrafts aren't a particular forte of the Team Sarashina members at present, were such skills to be required for their professional duties, they would set about acquiring them through extraordinary dedication and perseverance. It is precisely this aspect of the Sarashinas that earns them such acclaim.

In a sense, Team Sarashina's role is that of a rescue squad. If a major order comes in unexpectedly, they'll step in and lend a hand on the production line. They are also sent out to help with external projects. Some readers may be wondering if the Sarashinas are allotted the task of entertaining clients—that is, taking clients out to meals, bars, karaoke joints, and the like to ensure that business relations run smoothly—but I am happy to say that, unlike many other firms, our company has never engaged in such brain-dead practices.

Not that Team Sarashina's members are the only bright stars around here. Tsuyuko and Yoneko, the sales team's highest performers, revered for their ability to make people listen to them against their will, also command a lot of respect in the company. That said, they are known to have gone a little bit far on occasion, and just between you and me, they cause Mr. Tei a bit of a headache.

Often, when your eyes meet Tsuyuko's and Yoneko's, you find that the sweet that was in your hand a second ago is now in one of theirs, and so I make a policy of avoiding eye contact with them at all costs. Though there is a guy called Shigeru, who joined the company recently, who seems to be totally immune to their tricks. I'm not sure if it's simply because he's so out of it all the time or what. In any case, thanks to him, these days I often see Tsuyuko and Yoneko wearing somewhat frustrated expressions. I guess, in a way, Shigeru's immunity is also a kind of a skill.

Anyhow, I've strayed off topic a little, but what I was getting to was this: the main reasons that Team Sarashina are held up as the jewel in the company's crown are, first, their exceptional teamwork and, second, the extreme precision and speed with which they go about their designated tasks.

The projects that they have a hand in planning are always met with success. Each time they step up to the production line, they manage without fail to far surpass the standard run quantity, and, when they're sent out on location, they are received rapturously. The word that crops up time and time again in feedback reports from their external postings is *dependable*.

Team Sarashina is made up of ten members. Ms. Sarashina, the official team leader, is generally quite subdued, but is capable of complete transformation when the occasion demands. With her healthy doses of blusher, the ever-comical Ms. Iwahashi keeps team spirit lifted. Bastions of capability, Ms. Nogiku and Ms. Matsushima know how to get things done, while Ms. Tatsuta, Ms. Wakaba, Ms. Matsukaze, Ms. Tamazasa, and Ms. Tsuyushiba silently support them, and the group's eldest member, Ms. Tagoto, keeps a sharp-eyed watch over all of them. They're a wonderful team, and they wouldn't be the same without any one of their members.

However unexpected the situation they find themselves in, the Sarashinas always come across as calm and poised. I'm sure that nobody will disagree when I say that just the sight of the ten of them together, all wearing the same expression of perfect composure, is overwhelming enough to make a person surrender to them on the spot. Some companies we deal with still have their fair share of cocky types, or people going around sexually harassing others even though everyone knows that's not cool anymore, but when Team Sarashina make their entrance, those sorts tend to shrivel up and start behaving. If they don't, then Ms. Sarashina, who loathes injustice of any kind, will eventually lose it. I forgot to mention that Ms. Sarashina used to be something of a wild child, so she's very capable in that regard.

To this day, nobody has ever seen any of the Sarashinas in a state of panic.

Once, when the Sarashinas were in the factory, a mixing vat exploded owing to an error in the quantities of chemicals used. Nobody in the team batted an eyelid, and nobody said a word. In no time at all, the mess was cleared up and the line reopened.

The origin of the Sarashina team is a subject veiled in mystery. All kinds of theories are whispered among the other employees: some people think Ms. Tagoto was once the leader and that when she decided it was time for a new generation to take over, she recruited the other nine; others maintain that the present team have been there from its very inception. Nobody knows for sure. No one even knows when the team came into being. One day they were just there, doing all kinds of jobs at a mind-boggling pace. I'm sure it can't just be me who's intrigued by how they came to develop that incredible sense of unity.

It's not just in work matters that the Sarashinas are high achievers. Our company doesn't have its own sports teams or anything like that—although employees are actively encouraged to have hobbies, and many people go to Thai lessons or yoga classes on their days off or on their way home—but when we receive news of an intercompany tournament of some kind, we never let the opportunity pass us by. The information always gets relayed to Team Sarashina right away, because in the realm of the tournament, they are truly on home turf. There, the Sarashinas really have the chance to show people what they're made of.

Because they are experts in the art of teamwork, they have a natural aptitude for team sports. They are particularly talented at volleyball, and have won every intercompany volleyball tournament so far. Their determination during the match is so formidable, it's as if some kind of spectral energy is rising off them.

Of course, in its sporting formulation, Team Sarashina is still composed entirely of female members, but even when faced with a rival team that is mixed or all male, they emerge victorious. Though they won't say it explicitly, it's clear that they simply love to win, and they seem particularly jubilant when they beat a men's team. People still talk of the time when their rigid composure broke after thrashing a team of hulky men at basketball, and they beamed with joy. That was how people discovered that ten grinning Sarashinas actually make for quite an eerie spectacle. You just don't know what they're going to do.

On that occasion, someone called Ms. Sarashina as she was headed into the changing room, and somehow summoned the courage to ask her why she liked winning so much.

"We like showing people what we're capable of," she said calmly as she wiped away the sweat from her neck, and then she and the other Sarashinas filed into the changing room with supreme poise.

As it happens, the most recent intercompany championship wasn't a sports tournament, but a traditional Japanese dance competition. When I first heard about it, I assumed it would be a step too far even for Team Sarashina but they began to practice with astounding dedication right away, as if they'd been issued a challenge to which they were determined to rise. As soon as their work for the day had finished, they'd flock to the dancing school and rehearse for at least three hours. You couldn't help but admire their extraordinary effort. Where did they get this drive?

On the day of the competition, I set out excitedly for the hall where it was being held. Wielding skills I never knew she had, Ms. Nogiku danced a stunning solo, which was followed by a fan dance from Ms. Sarashina and Ms. Tagoto, who made quite the stellar duo. The other members, positioned around them onstage, sporting their usual composed expressions, joined in for the dazzling finale. When it was over, I applauded their accomplishments and their ethereal brilliance with all the gusto I had. I imagine there may be readers who think that because the Sarashinas have mastered Japanese dance, they'd be an asset for entertaining customers in a tatami room, geisha-style, but I am happy to report our company has never engaged in such brain-dead practices.

Unfortunately, this time the Sarashinas had to suffer the indignity of second place (first place was snatched up by an invincible team who'd been dancing for more than a decade). With no perceptible change of expression, they filed out of sight into the changing room. I can only imagine that their attempts next year will be even more determined. If anything, the display renewed my resolve to follow their progress as a devoted fan.

The picture below shows Team Sarashina standing with their customary composed expression in front of the shelf outside the company reception room, where a medley of trophies and certificates they've won are displayed.

A Day Off

I'm lying faceup on my bed right now. I did get up this morning—I ate breakfast and quickly vacuumed my apartment—but then I felt the urge to rest, and I've lain here since. I'm sprawled on top of my bedcover, a thin, Korean-made quilt that I bought online after falling in love with its pretty shade of violet-blue. The weather's about to turn cold, and soon I'll be needing a blanket at night. I'd better start looking for one. Then I'd better buy it.

The eruption of children's voices from the grade school next door must mean it's lunchtime. Honestly, the time just whizzes by. It's my day off, Wednesday is ladies' discount day at the cinema, and a part of me would like to go to see a movie, but the thought of leaving the house is so off-putting. It seems as though today is destined to be an off day. I'm not even properly dressed yet—I'm still lounging around in my Hanes blue sweatshirt. I wish the school would make me lunch too, in recognition of my living so close. It's been such a long time since I ate those stews and curries and other less easily categorized dishes from those aluminum bowls, and I'd love to do it again. Those weird vinegary salads they used to give us along with pickles and other stuff. Truth is, I really can't be bothered to make my own lunch, and I can't be bothered to go out to eat either.

Gum is sitting on my chest. That's a pretty frequent occurrence, so I can't recall the exact moment when she jumped up there, the toes of both her feet arranged in a neat little row. She's perched in the exact spot where, if my chest were a bit more voluminous, travelers would start to feel concerned about the cleft in the terrain stretching out ahead of them. As it is, though, my chest seems to shrink with every passing year, so any visitors to the area would probably only feel disappointment at the lack of adventure on offer.

Gum is staring fixedly in my direction, but it's not like she wants anything in particular. She's just staring. It's only Gum who looks at me this way. When humans stare at other humans like this, it ends up taking on a certain significance, so we tend not to.

A gurgling sound escapes from Gum's throat. I like it when she's sitting like this—it feels intimate somehow. Gum looks pretty relaxed, but of course she's not putting her whole weight on me. If she did, I'm sure I'd be crushed to death instantly. As we gaze at each other in silence, Gum and I are thinking about totally different things. I'm thinking about Mr. Ōya.

I haven't known Mr. Ōya for very long. In fact, we had our first date just the other day. It's still a bit early to tell, but I think he's probably a really great guy. If someone were to ask me what makes him different from other people, I don't think I could answer. I wonder if he actually is any different from other people. He and I both—we're just humans, right? But no, something about him must be different. There must be something that sets him apart.

I stroke Gum's back and ponder exactly what is distinctive about Mr. Ōya. Gum narrows her round eyes. It seems she's enjoying being stroked.

The thing I like most about Mr. Ōya is how calm

he is. I also like that his hands aren't overly big or small, and I like the clothes he wears. There's something about his presence I find reassuring. But what does that all mean? None of these qualities are particularly extraordinary, and they can't explain the things I'm feeling.

From outside the window, I can hear the loudspeakers announcing that it's cleaning time at the school, and then a crackly nursery rhyme starts to play.

Words like *love* and *romance* make no sense at all to me. It's a terrifying thought that for such a long time, the continuation of the human race has relied on such ill-defined, potentially illusory concepts. If you ask me, it's everything that has happened in the past that's abnormal. The dwindling birth rate seems to me a total inevitability. It's as if everyone's finally woken up to the reality of our situation. When things get really bad, we can perish side by side. Rather than forcing people to have babies, better that we all just die together.

"Right, Gum?" I scratch a spot on the right side of Gum's chin. She cocks her head, entreating me to scratch the other side too, so I obey.

I'm not very good with that half-pleasurable,

half-sickening feeling you get when you're about to fall for someone, or when you're in the process of falling for someone little by little. I also suspect that I just like the feeling of having someone to obsess over, rather than actually liking him that much as a person. I've been guilty of the same thing in the past. Plus, just because you like someone doesn't necessarily mean it's a romantic kind of liking. Nothing in the various love and dating guides I've read has ever really struck a chord with me, and romantic movies and novels don't either. I've just never been moved by stories of love and passion, so what I'm experiencing now makes even less sense. Are love and romance meant for me, or not? That's what I'd like to know.

I shut my eyes, and the warm light filtering through my Indian cotton curtains hits my eyelids. I can feel Gum's breath on my chin. She breathes really hard through her nose. The force of it splits my bangs, parting the hair to either side of my forehead. It tickles.

Gum and I grew up together. When she was a baby, Gum was absolutely tiny. I used to pick her up between my index finger and thumb and place her on my kid-size hand, and there she would wriggle around, working her way along its creases. It tickled so much that I couldn't keep from laughing. Back then, I never once imagined she'd grow to this kind of size.

I named her Gum because the cold dampness of her body and her sticky mucus most closely resembled a ball of chewed-up gum. In the very beginning, I used to call her Croaky—not very original, I know. But then I hit on Gum, which seemed just perfect to me, and Gum herself seemed to like it too. So that's what I called her, all the time we were growing up together. I always looked out for Gum, as if I were her older sister.

When I got to middle school, I started to realize what a valuable presence Gum was. Once, when my after-school club had dragged on for a long while and I was walking home in the dark, I saw a man dressed in black, hiding behind a utility pole. I was terrified, but I summoned Gum and she came to my aid right away. In university, too, Gum helped me deal with a senior guy who wouldn't leave me alone.

My friends were having similar experiences. Such things happened day in and day out, working their way into our lives as if they had every right to be there. Sitting around in the student canteen, eating my cheese katsu and listening to my friends talking about being groped on the train, I would desperately wish that everyone had a Gum of their own. Gum has protected me through everything.

That's why now Gum and I work to protect everyone else. We provide support for women facing problems with groping, stalking, harassment, and other kinds of abuse. It's the perfect job for us. When women are on the move or coming home from work, I'll either walk with them or watch over them from a distance. Sometimes, I'm on stakeout duty. It never takes too long for the men who like to cause trouble to show up. Then I summon Gum, and Gum and I glare at the men, and they flee. They scatter like little baby spiders. After years of being bosom buddies, Gum and I are now also a professional dream team.

Sometimes we come across bullish types who aren't shooed away quite so easily, but when Gum opens her mouth wide, revealing her long tongue, which could easily lasso a person or two, they lose their nerve immediately. Some experience a loss of consciousness. Some experience a loss of continence. With such pathetic opponents, there's no need for Gum to really exert herself. Thinking about it, I've never seen Gum really exert herself. She just sits there, quietly, observing human society, with all that potential hidden away inside her huge body. Possibly, she's just dumbstruck by the utter mess we're all in.

To be honest, there seems to be no end to these vile men incapable of controlling their sexual impulses. The demand for people in our line of work is incredibly high. Our company insists that we take two full days off a week, but even on such days I find myself thinking about all the poor women in trouble somewhere out there. That's why recently I've been suggesting to our department head, Kuzuha, that we put on classes teaching people how to draw magic circles as a means of self-protection. Say what you want, but the people best prepared for dire situations common to this world are those who know how to draw magic circles.

I guess if I'm totally honest, I'm getting a bit sick of staring down men with Gum. I'm think I'm just over it. What I'd like most of all is if Gum and I and whoever else could all just hang out together and smile and have a good time. I definitely don't fancy the idea of having glaring matches with Mr. Ōya. And when I think about all the things that have happened in my life up until now and that have happened to all other women, I know living in a state of total harmony just isn't going to happen. That makes me sad. In fact, it makes me incredibly sad, and incredibly angry, makes me wilt right there on the spot—and that's why I have no desire to leave my bedroom, where I can just loll around with Gum like this.

Gum is still sat on my chest, staring at me. Maybe she's hungry. I'm hungry too, Gum. The grade school next door has fallen silent again. I guess the afternoon lessons must have started already. The lime-green curtains sway gently from side to side. In Gum's black eyes, I can see my reflection—the reflection of a woman who has lost faith in the idea of men.

I pat Gum's head with its straight, narrow nose, and Gum arches her brown back with its stylish black marking, revealing her eggshell-colored underbelly running from the base of her neck all the way down to her stomach. Her nose is slimy. Gum is pretty slimy all over, actually.

I don't know if she's had a change of mood or if she couldn't bear her hunger pangs anymore, but with as little perceptible reason as when she first climbed on me, Gum dismounts and disappears in the direction of the kitchen. I'm left lying on the bed, my sweatshirt now covered in sticky Gum slime. Keeping up with the washing is no joke when you live with an enormous toad.

No longer buried by Gum's large stomach, my smaller stomach growls loudly, as if crying out for joy at being liberated.

I can see there's nothing for it—I'm going to have to find something to eat. With a big groan, I hoist myself up from the bed.

Having a Blast

The idea of waiting *three whole years* for my hair to grow out is nuts. I can't deny that when I'm scaring people, it'd help accentuate the mood somewhat if my hair was all long and disheveled, but with such a range of wigs and other options on offer these days, waiting all that time would just be dumb.

When I died, which was a pretty long time ago, it was customary to shave dead people's heads. I woke up in the afterlife lamenting the loss of my hair, which I'd treasured more than life itself—although I was already lifeless at that point, so I don't know how that works! Anyway, as I tremulously made my way to the

River of Three Crossings in that white shroud they'd dressed me in and peeked at my reflection, I saw that my shiny bald pate kind of suited me. That really took me aback. I never noticed it while I was alive, but I have quite a nicely shaped skull.

While I was alive, the idea that my husband would remarry after my death left me devastated and distraught, but as soon as I actually died, I stopped caring. It was as if whatever fear or anxiety had been possessing me had slipped right out of my body. People assume that ghosts must be up to their eyes in resentment and all, but that's a misperception. I feel as if I had a lot more grudges when I was alive than I do now.

While we were still together, my husband used to say that if he ever remarried, I ought to come back to haunt him if he took another wife—so I decided to make an appearance. His remarriage happened slightly sooner than I was expecting, but I guess that's how it goes. He'd always been incapable of doing anything alone, so it figured. An image of my mother-in-law desperately rushing to find a new wife for her darling only son flashed through my head. When I'd fallen sick, she'd seemed truly distressed.

It was going to take a full three years before my hair got to a decent length even in this dimension, and as I said at the beginning, that seemed ludicrous to me, so I decided to make an appearance in all my bald glory. Full disclosure: I've always been a real lazy-bones. While I was alive, I made a brave effort to hide my true nature, but now that I'm dead, I behave exactly as I please.

It had been a while since I'd been back to our house, but barely a thing had changed. In fact, the only alteration was that the person lying next to my husband on the thin futon was not me. The new wife was fast asleep. I couldn't see her face, and I didn't make a huge effort to look, either. I reached out a hand and tapped my ex-husband's shoulder. He opened his eyes immediately.

I thought he might get a fright seeing me there with my bald head and all, but he just burst out laughing.

"Man, it really suits you!"

(Of course, my husband is from a different era, so he didn't actually use these words. Translated into modern parlance, though, this is what he meant.)

I rubbed my head bashfully—bald heads feel great to rub—and smiled.

"You saw it at the funeral too, though."

"Yeah, but I wasn't really in a position to notice that kind of thing. I just felt so awful."

"Aww, thanks. That's sweet of you. Well, as you can see, I'm not doing badly at all, so I want you to enjoy yourself as well, okay?"

"Okay, that's cool."

"See you, then."

"'Bye for now."

And with that, we parted again. I think that was a better parting than our first one. The first time around, I'd been at death's door, and then I'd died, and between all the caring for me and the grief and so on, my husband was a total mess. Come to think of it, I think we were both intoxicated by the tragedy that had befallen us. From where I'm standing now, that seems totally uncool.

Anyway, from that point on, I've kept my shaved head. I've seen a lot of styles of dress come and go across the ages, but I feel like today's fashion is probably best suited to the buzzcut look. There are lots of women like me on earth these days—their ears full of piercings, wearing ripped band T-shirts and torn black jeans, Doc Martens, bright red lipstick and plenty of eyeliner. It seems like people have finally caught up with my style. What took them so long? That's what I'd like to know.

I'm pretty partial to this age from a cultural

perspective, too. I guess the correct term is "pop cul-ture"? Anyway, I like it. I find myself listening to loads of music and watching a ton of films. This year I was very proud to see that Furiosa in *Mad Max: Fury Road* had the same haircut as I do. I was so pleased, in fact, that I ended up going to see it four times! I kept on pop-ping up in the aisle, on the seats and in various other places around the auditorium, cheering Furiosa on in her adventures, stealing bits of caramel-coated pop-corn and slurps of Coke from audience members too caught up in the action to notice. That was a real blast.

My wife seems to be enjoying herself so much after death that I haven't yet managed to speak to her.

This is my first wife I'm talking about here. She was of a sickly disposition while she was alive and passed away in no time at all after we married. In fact, the postmortem version of her seems more full of life than the living one ever did.

Nowadays we're both working at the same com-pany. It's a big company and she seems entirely obliv-ious to the fact that I work here, too. There are times when I think to myself, surely, surely she must have seen me just then? The other day, we passed right by each other in the corridor, but she was wearing these huge headphones carelessly leaking sound, and she walked right past me, humming. It's not like she's ignoring me deliberately. She's a punk these days, so she doesn't make eye contact with or smile at everyone she passes. I want to respect that choice. Above all, I'm just happy that she seems to be doing well.

Now I can understand what she might have been thinking when she came to visit me when I was still alive, stood by my bed, and told me in a very phlegmatic way that she was doing fine, and that she wanted me to enjoy my life just as she was enjoying her death, before promptly disappearing. At the time, it struck me as a bit coldhearted. I wanted her to be pining for me, forever and ever. Remembering that now, it seems pretty damn rich of me to have felt that way when my new wife was lying right there beside me in bed.

My wife belongs to one of the company's top-secret departments, and the nature of her job is shrouded in mystery. Mine, on the other hand, consists of regular admin work and routine checks.

I don't have any exceptional talents. After my death, I came to see that very clearly. It made me wonder what on earth I'd been playing at while I was still alive. People treated me well because I was a man—they treated me the way that men were treated. They sorted out a new marriage for me right away when my first wife died, and generally made sure everything was hunky-dory. I took that for granted, and while I'm embarrassed to admit it, I never really gave it much thought. I don't even remember having worked particularly hard. What was I thinking, honestly?

But I like my current job. Maybe it's just a reaction against the brainless existence I led while I was alive, but this steady work that demands persistence and accuracy is novel to me, and even enjoyable. I always wanted to do things properly. I really did.

At our company, there's about a fifty-fifty split between the living and the dead. There are also a few who occupy a kind of intermediary position between the two. Of course, most of the living can't see us dead. My guess is that if they could, they'd be genuinely shocked by how many people are moving around this building.

Since I joined this company I've often thought about how people tend to be much more full of beans after they die. That definitely goes for my first wife. The living have this great limitation placed on them by the fact they could kick the bucket at any time. Having a mortal body is really restrictive. What's more, you've got society to deal with, which restricts you even further. I feel genuinely sorry for humans. I don't mean to make excuses for myself, but I do feel that society had a role to play in what a waste of space I was while alive—although back then I'm not sure they even had a word for what I'm describing as society.

After lunch one day, I was sitting on a bench in the courtyard drinking a can of coffee when I glimpsed Mr. Tei walking down one of the first-floor corridors. No sooner had that perception formulated itself in my mind than he was standing right in front of me. It scared me half to death. Mr. Tei does stuff like that, though. He shows up everywhere, and gets through an unbelievable amount of work, to the extent that what he does often seems physically impossible.

"Agh! Mr. Tei! Honestly, how many of you are there?" I once said jokingly.

"Oh, there's only one of me," he replied, deadly serious. "How is work going?"

"I'm enjoying it," I answered honestly, a big smile breaking across my face.

"That's good to hear."

I thought I saw the corners of his mouth relax slightly at this, but he was still just as expressionless as ever.

"How about you, Mr. Tei?"

"What do you mean?"

"What does work really mean for you? How much importance do you place on company mottoes and business models and things like that?" I said, deciding on the spur of the moment to try out some of the terminology from a best-selling business book I'd just finished reading.

"Company mottoes and business models . . ." I saw a frown form beneath Mr. Tei's black-rimmed spectacles. "Well, personally I think that the first priority is to squeeze as much as you can from the rich."

As I reeled slightly at the unexpectedly militant tone of his answer, Mr. Tei continued. "Then to give it back to the poor, in whatever ways you can. The imbalance between the rich and the poor has always troubled me profoundly."

With that, Mr. Tei bowed to me and headed off toward the main gates. I noticed he was suddenly sporting a cozy wool scarf and carrying a briefcase, neither of which, I was sure, he'd had a moment ago. What a peculiar character, I thought to myself as I drained the tepid dregs of coffee from the can.

•

My husband seems to be really enjoying his work after death, so I watch over him quietly. While he was alive, he used to leave absolutely everything to me, so the change is really heartening. Thinking about it now, I probably should have challenged his behavior more at the time—should have questioned whether he really thought it was okay to act like that, and thought more about my rights and so on—but back then I didn't have the slightest issue with it. More fool the both of us.

I should explain that my husband isn't a bad sort really. I don't have a problem with talking to him per se. It just feels a bit boring to have the same kind of relationship in the afterlife as we had while alive, and at the moment I reckon things are just fine as they are. Acting all lovey-dovey requires effort, anyway.

Standing by the window, sipping my drink through a straw, I look down on my husband as he sits on a bench in the courtyard. With all the shrinking and expanding that goes on, the geography of this company is hard to wrap one's head around as it is, but the section where I work is tucked away in a particularly out-of-the-way corner of the building, so there's little risk of my being found out. I'm not permitted to divulge too much about the nature of the work I do, but broadly speaking, I'm in research and development.

Sometimes I wish that my talents were a bit more interesting—that I could metamorphose or had some other special skill at my disposal like the company's star players have—but I also know there's no use longing for something you don't have. I'm satisfied with what I've got. Bringing new things into the world is an amazing occupation. I'm also thoroughly attached to the lab coat I have to wear here. I don't know why, but this white coat just really suits me.

Now that I'm dead, the husband I loved so much seems like a total stranger. That's been a major revelation. In my case, my husband died before I did, so I got to fully savor the joys of single life for a while again before my own death. I guess that didn't help matters.

For the record, I'd like to state that I did go through a proper grieving period. For a time, I spent every evening weeping, asking myself why he'd had to go and leave me on my own. But at some point, I realized that it was actually easier being alone. It also meant a lot less housework.

So maybe it's a bit of an exaggeration to say that I'm "watching over" him. He just happens to fall into my field of vision—that's about the size of it. By the look of things, he hasn't spoken to his first wife either, so he probably has a similar take on matters. That all's fine and dandy, it seems to me. Everyone's enjoying themselves, everyone's happy, so where's the problem?

I watch him toss his empty coffee can in the trash and return to work as I enjoy the last of my sweet and delicious Starbucks iced chai latte. Even though the weather's taken a wintry turn, I still far prefer them iced.

The Missing One

"One, two, three, four . . ."

Outside the window a bicycle raced from right to left, its bell ringing cheerfully, and for a second Kikue almost lost track of her count, but she managed to focus her efforts and resumed.

"Five, six, seven, eight, nine . . ."

Kikue took her hands off the plates and stretched them above her head. This was her third attempt to count the plates.

"Nope, there really is one missing here," she murmured to herself. She checked the stock sheet just to be sure, but it was marked with an unambiguous "10." Kikue stared at the nine plates laid out in front of her on the counter. She'd loved them the moment she first laid eyes on them at the trade show last year. Seeing those pretty drawings of plants and animals, she'd felt her heart rate quicken. They were proving to be a hit with the customers too. As soon as Kikue posted news on her blog and her Instagram account that the plates were in stock, people would start appearing from goodness knows where, walking away with their favorite piece from the selection. It was fair to say they were the shop's most popular product. Because they were hand-painted individually by an up-and-coming illustrator, the plates took a while to be delivered, which only fueled people's passion further. And now, when Kikue's order had finally arrived after such a long wait, one of them was missing.

Returning to their boxes the plates she'd been intending to put straight out onto the shelves, Kikue opened her laptop and typed an email to the person she'd been in touch with at the manufacturing company:

> *Unfortunately, the shipment we received today is missing an item.*

As she hit the send button, Kikue let out a deep sigh. Writing these kinds of emails always made her a bit tense. Manufacturers quite often refused to take her seriously, or listen to what she was saying, because she was a woman single-handedly running a shop. In that respect, at least, owning a shop wasn't that different to office life. She'd only interacted with this particular company over email, and the one thing she knew about the person she'd been in touch with was that he was a man. She could tell by his name: Yūta. She just had to hope that he believed her.

You sure about that, love? an imaginary middle-aged man admonished Kikue in her head. *Sure you didn't just break it? Think you can pull the wool over our eyes, do you?* With lewd eyes, the man glared at her mockingly.

In order to preemptively alleviate the shock she would feel if something really terrible happened, Kikue chose to imagine the worst-case scenario. This habit of insuring herself in advance, of building a protective wall around herself, had been firmly established by the time she entered her mid-thirties.

Would this Yūta be that kind of a man? Kikue asked herself as she stared at his name on the screen. Well, even if he was, she'd already imagined the worst so she wouldn't be surprised, and she wouldn't be hurt.

Kikue closed her laptop and set about arranging the

other items from the shipment, which she'd checked and found no problems with. It was a small shop, the size of just eight tatami mats, with built-in wooden shelves lining the walls on either side. In the middle was a large wooden table arranged with ceramics and linen items, and at the rear the counter with the cash register, behind which Kikue spent most of her time. She'd painted the plaster walls white, back when she first opened the shop. At first, she'd thought they might be a bit too white, but by now the color had lost its glare and looked rather good. It was the same with Himeji Castle, which you could see wherever you were in this town—when its renovations had finished, people had been variously worried or up in arms about how white it looked, but now, two years on, the color had toned down and it was just right. The same went for everything in life: you had to give things some time before you could be really sure about them.

The section of wall closest to the shop window jutted out slightly, offsetting the balance of the whole space. It caused Kikue a lot of concern, but there was nothing she could do about it. Behind the protuberance lay the concrete beam holding up the monorail. The Himeji Monorail had officially shut down the year that Kikue was born, although in fact it hadn't been running for several years prior to that. Kikue had never once ridden it, and yet it was an integral part of her everyday life.

The monorail had opened in the 1960s, and for a period of just eight years had run the mile-long stretch from Himeji Station westward to Tegarayama. The brevity of its lifespan stood to reason. A mile was an eminently walkable distance. Because it was an eminently walkable distance, and because monorail tickets were expensive, everyone walked. When Kikue had learned about it as an adult, it had sounded to her like a bad joke. What on earth had the mayor been thinking?

Tegarayama was home to an aquarium, a botanical garden, and a cultural center familiar to locals who had taken classes of any kind. All of Himeji's recitals took place there. Kikue had learned piano until middle school, and had taken part in several recitals held at the center. To get there, you just had to follow the trail of columns holding up the monorail track. Although it seemed scarcely believable, it was in fact true: even after the monorail was shut down, the tracks had remained there untouched for decades because pulling them down would have been too costly. If the Good Witch of the North had lived in Himeji, it wouldn't have been the yellow brick road she'd have been telling people to follow, but the vestiges of the monorail.

With those columns dotted around, there was never any fear of anyone getting lost.

Kikue had left Himeji at the end of her teenage years to attend university in another part of the country and had subsequently found a job at a company in Osaka. Her family home was on the north side of the castle, so even on her occasional visits back to the city, she'd rarely ventured out to the monorail part of town where her shop now stood.

The shop had once been a makeup salon run by Kikue's mother. It was the kind of place you often found in shopping arcades in rural towns, where local women came to get cosmetic advice and buy products. In Kikue's childhood memories, the little salon was always spilling over with middle-aged women.

When her mother told her over the phone that she'd decided to close the salon, Kikue didn't feel a moment's hesitation. She didn't have a lot of savings, but she knew the rent for this shop was ridiculously cheap. If she moved back in with her mother, she calculated, her rent would be lower than it was for her Osaka apartment.

And so Kikue quit her job, redecorated the place—doing as much of the work as she could by herself—and started her own gift shop. She'd had enough of working for companies that were far too big. Kikue wanted to feel on top of everything that was going on around her. And if things didn't work out? Well, then she'd figure out then and there what to do next.

Still, when Kikue had gone back to the shop for the first time in years and seen that monorail column skewering the place, she half doubted her eyes. "What the . . . ?" she found herself muttering under her breath. It was far more peculiar than she remembered it. To add insult to injury, the building had aged considerably too.

The entire block on which Kikue's shop stood—a rather dreary strip of stores, including a ramen restaurant and a hair salon, all of which were exactly the same shape and size—was punctuated at regular intervals by monorail columns that poked up from the buildings like tall chimneys. Right there on the other side of the street was a block of slick-looking new apartments with auto-locking doors, but here, it was as if time had ground to a halt.

If you headed west from where the strip of shops ended you came to the Takao Apartments, which contained on one of its lower floors the platforms for the Daishogun Monorail Station. The apartments were no longer occupied and had fallen into ruin. Vines and leaves had grown across the beams, so they looked like the limbs of giant monsters.

If you crossed the road instead, making your way past the convenience store and the apartment blocks under construction, you reached the bank of the Senba River. Here, too, you would find monorail columns and tracks dotting the landscape. In this part of the city, through which the San'yō shinkansen ran, residents had done more or less as they pleased with the monorail tracks—affixing them with signs that read NO ILLEGAL DUMPING, growing morning glories along them, planting herbs and vegetables in the space around, and so on. Doubtless the transformation had happened gradually, over a long stretch of time. It was all a very strange business, and what Kikue found strangest was that growing up, it had never once occurred to her how bizarre those monorail remains were. She supposed there were things that became visible only when you left a place, grew older.

Not long after Kikue moved back to Himeji, an ex-boyfriend of hers from Osaka had taken the day off work and come to visit her, and the pair had strolled along the monorail tracks to the aquarium. Although they'd already broken up, they dawdled that short distance hand in hand.

It had been a cloudy day, Kikue remembered. Her ex had read up online about the monorail before coming and he seemed genuinely excited by its existence, taking a load of photos. When Kikue had asked him that morning where he wanted to visit, he'd said it was the monorail he wanted to see, rather than the castle, which was by far Himeji's favored tourist attraction.

The disused monorail had a certain popularity among those with a penchant for railways and ruins and so on. Kikue was now used to seeing people coming and going in front of her shop with big cameras slung around their necks. Some even stood outside the window and peered in covetously. She knew instantly that their dreamy gaze was directed not at the carefully curated merchandise on display but at the protruding section in the wall concealing the column. The tracks had been dismantled little by little over the last few decades, but with proper demolition work now finally getting under way, many people wanted to pay the monorail a final visit. It was very possible that in the future, this block containing Kikue's shop would be knocked down entirely. It was also highly plausible that the real reason behind Kikue's ex's visit was a wish to see the monorail while he still had the chance.

With her ex, Kikue visited the aquarium for the first time in decades. The aquarium stood at a height aboveground, and her ex surprised her with the information that its entrance had once been the last station on the monorail line. She'd had no idea.

From a walkway leading to the aquarium, they looked down at the route they'd just walked and the spot where the line of monorail columns broke off for the final time. It was easy to surmise the course that the now-phantom monorail had traced from there to here during the days of its existence. The idea that its destination was still standing while its midway section was gone struck Kikue as kind of sad. The monorail was like the town's phantom limb. Its loss was felt. It was only when all of it was gone that people would cease to be aware of its absence and stop missing it.

For anyone used to big city aquariums like Osaka's Kaiyukan, as Kikue and her ex were, the Tegarayama aquarium was utterly unspectacular, yet there were several displays that left them baffled. The one that particularly floored them both was the Specimen Corner. There was the exhibit labeled DECAPITATED GREAT SALAMANDER, which, true to its description, was a great headless salamander in formaldehyde. This was displayed alongside the CANNIBALIZED GREAT SALAMANDER, with half of its body eaten away. The panel under the latter read as follows:

In 1996, one of our great salamanders,
35 cm in length, was eaten by another
large salamander, 117 cm, in the tank
and then regurgitated.

When they stepped away from the Specimen Corner, Kikue's ex said with a stunned expression, "I feel like I've been permanently scarred."

Kikue, who felt exactly the same, nodded gravely. The Petting Corner, where as a youngster she had touched starfish and various little fishes, now had a large pool containing sharks and flatfish. Several signposts warned WE CAN BITE! in red lettering.

Afterward, they visited the botanical gardens, which had an oddly extensive selection of insectivorous plants. The explanations accompanying the hand-drawn illustrations were unsettling. Kikue could remember being entranced by the shy plants they had there in her childhood, which would shrink from her touch by curling up their leaves. The botanical gardens were far more run-down and neglected than she recalled.

"Your hometown is kind of weird," said her ex with a chuckle as they made their way back along the monorail tracks toward the station. Kikue agreed. It was as though the city channeled every last drop of its sublime energy into Himeji Castle. Accordingly, everywhere else was somehow a bit . . . off. Kikue was glad that she'd been able to share that weirdness with her ex, which she'd sensed since she was young. In the end, though, they remained apart, even though Osaka and Himeji weren't really that far away from each other.

A woman entered, and Kikue bobbed her head in greeting. Realizing that the shop was deathly silent, she hurriedly pressed play on her iPod, and Blossom Dearie's honeyed tones flooded out of the speakers. Kikue had discovered since opening her shop that the owner of a gift shop ended up playing "gift-shop music" without ever intending to.

With rough, careless movements, the woman picked up a wooden spoon and a couple of mugs and inspected them, then walked out of the shop. Kikue felt a pang in her chest. Although she had spent her time watching her mother at work, it was only now, when Kikue had a shop of her own, that she realized what a sociable person her mother was, how good she had been with the customers. Nowadays, Kikue's mom spent her days absorbed in foreign TV drama series.

The truth was, Kikue still couldn't get used to the fact that complete strangers could simply stroll in off the street to this sanctuary that she had created. Of course, she understood that that was the very definition of a shop. She knew she had to stand there with her heart wide open and declare, "Here you go! This is me! Come take a look, and then leave again whenever you like!" but she also knew it was going to take her some time before she could manage it. Come to think of it, there were plenty of people running cafés and bookshops on their own who were either downright unfriendly or just not very good at dealing with people. Kikue figured that they must have set up their own shops because they disliked working in offices with other people. It made perfect sense. Kikue didn't think she'd fared too badly as a fully functioning member of society but she was, by nature, an introvert.

It was just beginning to get dark outside when the man entered. Kikue was crouched behind the counter, hiding herself away so as to drink tea from her stainless-steel flask. The flask had been advertised for its exceptional heat retention, and sure enough, the tea it stored was still steaming hot. Flustered by the arrival of a customer at such a moment, Kikue gulped down her tea and proceeded to choke violently. When she finally managed to collect herself and look up, she saw the man standing on the other side of the counter, peering down at her apologetically. Hurriedly, Kikue stood up.

"What can I do for you?" she said, her voice coming out hoarse and strange. "Sorry to give you a fright." Saying this, the man handed her a thick paper bag. "I'm from the plate company. I'm really sorry about the missing plate. It was our mistake. Would you mind just checking if this is the right one?"

Opening the bag, Kikue took out the flat cardboard box. Inside the box was a plate with various animals and plants trailing around the rim. Kikue smiled happily.

"Yes, this is the one. I love these plates. They're so pretty . . . but not *too* pretty, if you know what I mean."

The man smiled. "I'm really glad you think so. I'll pass your compliments on to the illustrator. I'm sure it'll make her day. My apologies again. Oh, I should have introduced myself at the start, shouldn't I? Anyway, thank you for doing business with us."

The business card he handed her was emblazoned with a name she had seen often in her in-box. So, Kikue thought, this is the famous Yūta.

She looked straight at the man standing in front of her. With his checked shirt and navy trousers, he gave off a soft, gentle impression. His short hair was flecked with white. Having imagined him as excessively awful, Kikue was now somewhat flummoxed at finding him quite the opposite.

"Oh, no, thank you. It's nice to meet you finally," Kikue said. She opened the drawer and pulled out one of her business cards, which she handed to him hesitantly. It was a long time since she'd given anyone a business card, and she had half-forgotten the etiquette.

Yūta took the card from Kikue, then said with a smile, "Your emails have always really intrigued me. I mean, you're living in Himeji, and the character in your name is the same as in Okiku's!"

Then, looking flustered, he went on, "I don't mean that in a bad way, of course. I'm kind of into ghost stories, you see."

Kikue smiled compassionately. "It's okay, I'm used to it. People often remark on it. When I was small, we'd often take school trips to Himeji Castle, and every time we'd pass the Okiku Well on the way to the exit, all the kids would laugh and call me Okiku."

Kikue hadn't minded having a name similar to the ghost in the story, or even being teased about it.

If anything, she was kind of proud to share one of the characters in her name with Okiku. The reason was simple: Okiku was incredibly popular. Visitors on their way out of Himeji Castle could be guaranteed to flock around the Okiku Well, peering inside it and raising their voices in excitement. It was almost unheard of to see a person walk straight past. Whatever they might have said about her, everyone knew who Okiku was, and there was something about that well that people found impossible to ignore. Her popularity was so great that it was surprising they hadn't started selling Okiku merchandise in the castle gift shop. It seemed rather special to Kikue that the legendary well, which she had always considered a fictional element in a story, really existed in the city. The Okiku Well brought together the unremarked and the remarkable. It was kind of amazing.

"I can imagine. I'm from Himeji too, so."

"Oh, really?"

"Our offices are in Kobe, but I commute from here. I'm just heading home now, so I thought I'd drop in on the way. I mean, I am genuinely sorry that there was a plate missing, but you know, with you being Kikue and this being a plate, I found it impossible to resist . . ."

Yūta smiled at her, laugh lines appearing around

the corners of his eyes. Reflexively, Kikue found herself stealing a glance at his left hand to check for the presence of a ring—even though she knew that many married people these days didn't wear wedding bands, and it really meant nothing.

"Also, did you know that the Okiku shrine is just around here?" he said.

"The Okiku shrine? No, I had no idea."

"I guess most people don't know about it, even those who live in the area. It's just a tiny little shrine, right over there. It's really worth a visit. They've got a gravestone for her, with the words *resolute woman* engraved on it."

"'Resolute woman'?"

"Yes, that's what it says. Kind of cool, right? I can show you one day, if you'd like. Not that it's far enough that you'd need showing especially, but I like it there, and I'd love you to see it."

"Oh, um, well, yes, that'd be great." In an attempt to compose herself, Kikue moved the box Yūta had brought over to where the other plates were stacked and began to count them again in jest.

"One, two . . ."

In an eerie voice, Yūta started counting along with her. "Three, four, five . . ."

Smiling, Kikue went on, more playfully than before. "Six, seven, eight, nine . . ."

Their eyes met, and together they said, "Ten!"

Their peals of laughter echoed through the little shop.

Kikue locked up the shop and set off east with Yūta, pushing her bike. They had carried on chatting until, before she knew it, it had been time for her to close up for the day. Her encounter with Yūta had been a bolt from the blue, but Kikue figured that such things could happen to anyone at any time and decided not to be surprised by it. When they emerged onto the main road, Kikue bade goodbye to Yūta, who was headed south. She got on her bike and made her way north. They had already made arrangements for their next meeting.

As Kikue pedaled away, Himeji Castle loomed ever larger in front of her. Kikue gazed up at the castle glowing so white in the sky, her cheeks now tinged a vivid red.

On High

Tomihime gazed down at the castle town spread out beneath her with an expression of utter boredom. She was so high up that despite the windows on all four sides being covered in mesh, she could see far off into the distance whatever the weather happened to be doing. From the south-facing window, she could see the honmaru and ni-no-maru—the innermost and secondary citadels. Past the moat was the main road that led to Himeji Station and, beyond that, a strip of distant sea. Tomihime knew this scene like the back of her hand. There was nothing even remotely arresting about it. Looking up at the blue sky, where the clouds and the factory smoke coexisted amicably, Tomihime let out a big yawn.

The castle was filled with the footsteps of visitors wearing the Himeji Castle slippers they had been given at the entrance. *Shuffle shuffle shuffle*, they went. Tomihime listened to the endless, sluggish sound with disgust. *Shuffle shuffle shuffle. Shuffle shuffle shuffle.* This was what it was like all year round, from the moment the castle gates opened in the morning to the moment they closed in the evening. It had become particularly bad since the renovations had finished; everyone was desperate to catch a glimpse of the castle's new look.

In retrospect, the renovation period had been blissfully quiet. The workmen had gone about their job with care, and the castle had been entirely shrouded in protective cloth for the duration. Tomihime had felt sufficiently at ease for the first time in ages, and had popped off to visit her younger sister, Kamehime.

To separate those on their way up from those going down, the castle corridors had been divided with cones and poles in red and green to indicate which routes the visitors should take, and there were separate staircases depending on whether you were ascending or descending, all of which effectively prevented any one spot becoming mobbed with tourists and—well, there was no denying that it had all been carefully thought out, but Tomihime refused to feel impressed in the slightest. Men and women, young and old, from all across the globe, speaking in myriad different languages, would praise the vista from the viewing deck of Tomihime's keep in the same way, take the same kinds of photos, then promptly disappear. Even after all that effort they had put into climbing the steep flight of stairs, they turned around and went padding back down almost immediately. Not a single person stopped to appreciate the fact that real people had once lived real lives in this place. Now even Tomihime found all of that hard to recall with any clarity. Was there any meaning to her still being here? Couldn't this lot be left to *shuffle shuffle shuffle* around on their own? In her heart of hearts, Tomihime felt like going and getting blind drunk.

Around closing time, when the numbers of visitors had eased considerably, a suited young man came up the stairs. Wearing a suit was clearly something he was not used to doing, and with everyone else around him dressed like tourists, he stuck out. Occasionally, there would be visitors who came to Himeji on business and had decided to stop by to look at the castle, but that didn't seem to be the case with this guy. When he caught sight of Tomihime sitting on the floor and leaning back against one of the columns in a manner not befitting a princess at all, he bowed and walked toward her.

Well, thought Tomihime, this is one for the books. It had been a long time since anyone had been able to see her.

The young man stopped short in front of Tomihime.

"Hello, my name is Shigeru Himekawa. I've recently taken over from Mr. Tei as the regional supervisor for this district, so I thought I'd stop by and introduce myself."

"Himekawa?" Tomihime stared at the man. In former times, men had wriggled and squirmed when Tomihime pinned them with her piercing gaze, but this young man showed no signs of doing so. Instead, he sat down very neatly beside Tomihime's outstretched legs and, with rather unseasoned movements, took out a business card and handed it to her.

Tomihime accepted it, although she really couldn't see the point in these white slips of paper. This would be the second one she owned now, the first having been given to her by Himekawa's predecessor, Mr. Tei. Tomihime had liked Mr. Tei. He was a pleasantly unmanly sort of man. Tomihime had always been drawn to men who stood out from the pack, with that dewy gleam in their eyes. Zushonosuke had been that type, too.

"Another guy with that name came up here, once, some time ago now. But it's just your name that's the same. You're not like him at all."

The young man's suit had clearly been purchased from a mass retailer, and it was on the cusp of being the wrong size. Something about the innocuousness of his attire gave him a shabby air. Poor guy, thought Tomihime.

"Really?" He cocked his head.

"Yeah, that guy risked his life to come up here. They all did, back then. They were petrified of us. I say 'us,' though, of course, there's only me now. Earlier, there were a few of us women here, and boy, were we something to see! We were unbeatable! Ach, those were the times. Those were my days of glory! You don't see guys staking their lives to climb up here now, that's for sure. They all put on those silly slipper things and come shuffling by. Do you know what I'm talking about? They're so loud, those slippers."

Seeing the disdain on Tomihime's face, the young man frowned. "Should I have risked my life to come up here? I think that could definitely be arranged, at least in terms of mental preparation. I'll remember that for next time."

Tomihime snorted. "Don't worry about it. It's just that everything felt really new back then, you know? We felt like we were special. I mean, we actually were special, and that felt great, but I'm over that now. Just come up normally, via the stairs. To be perfectly honest, I couldn't care less."

The young man winced. "You're still special, even now, Miss Tomihime. Mr. Tei has also been concerned that your morale has been low of late."

Tomihime eyed this new Himekawa sullenly. What had she done to deserve a visit from such a total dork? And when the old Himekawa had been so dreamy, too. If only they were in an open field right now, Tomihime thought, she would rip up a fistful of grass and throw it in this man's face.

"I wish you'd shut up! I'm still performing fine, okay? It's no easy task, you know, protecting a whole castle. And tell me, will you, what's the point of it? These days it's nothing more than a tourist attraction, pure and simple. I'm absolutely unnecessary, aren't I?"

At Tomihime's outburst, the young man frowned once more, directing his eyes up to the ceiling like a little boy posed with an impossible demand. Then he looked again at Tomihime.

"You're absolutely needed. The role of maintaining balance in a place, keeping things running smoothly, is an absolutely crucial one. Before making my way over here, I took a stroll around Himeji and what struck me was this: wherever you are in this town, you have a view of this castle. Whenever you go, you can look up and see it towering so beautifully above you. It's a most reassuring presence. In other words, Miss Tomihime, it's as if you are single-handedly protecting all the citizens of this city."

"Those are big claims."

"Yes."

Still glaring straight ahead, Tomihime shifted her legs and tucked them up beside her into a slightly neater arrangement. "So how come you can see me, anyway?"

The New Himekawa scratched his head. "Well, actually, my mother died not too long ago, and then for a time all kinds of strange things happened, then finally my mother started appearing to me."

"That's cool!"

The New Himekawa nodded seriously. "She said that in the beginning, she just wanted to avenge my father. But then, apparently, as she was figuring out how to perform scary stunts and practicing them, she realized what fun it was. She came to me because she wanted someone to whom she could show all her tricks to. Kind of like a magician."

"And that's how you came to see us?"

"At first I could only see my mother, actually. But she was always a really sociable person, a bit too sociable if you ask me, so it was only a matter of time before she started bringing along all these friends of hers from the ghost world. I told her a bunch of times not to bother because I couldn't see them, but she wasn't having any of it. She kept bringing them along and introducing them to me, totally convinced that I'd be able to see them, and then, sure enough, I started to be able to."

"Like a special education for a gifted child!"

"Yes, I suppose."

"And did Mr. Tei know about your gifts from the beginning?"

"No. Actually, all of this happened after I had started work at the company. I asked him the other day why he'd agreed to take me on. He said he just had a good feeling about me."

"Huh."

"Oh, and he also told me I seemed kind of dazed, which meant I wouldn't be overly affected by what was going on around me. He said he doesn't take on people who 'acclimatize too well to the age in which they're living.'"

"Right . . ." Tomihime stared at the New Himekawa with an expression that made no secret of what a weirdo she thought him to be, but he didn't recoil in the slightest.

Instead he said, "Well, I should get going. It's nearly closing time, and I just dropped by to make your acquaintance. But I'll be back."

As the New Himekawa lifted his skinny backside from the floor, Tomihime found herself getting to her feet too.

"Oh, come to think of it . . ." He glanced toward the south window, and then moved closer to it. "I was planning to drop by and say hello to Okiku too."

Standing side by side, Tomihime and the young man peered down. The Okiku Well, situated in the ni-no-maru, instantly entered their visual field. A number of people were crowded around it, peering down into its depths. Not too far off stood a security guard.

"She's not there, you know," Tomihime said, casually.

"What! Are you serious?" The New Himekawa's voice was a shrill cry. Tomihime plugged her fingers in her ears, feigning a wince. "Yeah, she left ages and ages ago. I guess it must have been sometime in the eighties? We discussed it all, before she left. You know what she's like—she's always been such a worrier. So she dropped by and asked me if I thought she'd stayed long enough. I reassured her that she'd done her time, and said I didn't mind at all, that she should go for it. Told her I'd take care of everything."

"I see! Still, that comes a bit of a disappointment, I must say."

"But you hadn't noticed, right? That's how it is with wells. And knowing that, I started to think that maybe the same goes for me. Maybe the castle would be perfectly fine without me being here. You know this idea that the dead will stay attached to this world, and be here forever? That's more or less just human arrogance. Okiku transmigrated, and now she's over there, doing very well for herself with that fine young man of hers."

Tomihime indicated a spot a little to the west of the station. Although there was no hope of him ever seeing where she was pointing, the New Himekawa squinted politely in the direction of Tomihime's finger.

"But the funny thing is, even after transmigrating, she's still there counting plates! I guess she's bound to them by destiny or whatever. Tomihime grinned, but the New Himekawa wasn't looking at her. He was looking between the well and the spot to the west, over and over, as if entranced. Finally, with a pained look on his face, he returned his gaze to Tomihime.

Tomihime opened her mouth and to her surprise found herself saying, without a smidgen of irony, "I mean, I'm fine to carry on for the time being."

The young man's face broke into a look of such intense joy that Tomihime felt spite resurfacing in her immediately. "But don't go thinking I'm going to hold out for your sake when I get really sick of it."

"No, of course," said the New Himekawa. "If and when that happens, let's get together and discuss our options." He nodded gravely several times.

A couple of hours after the young man disappeared down the stairs, night fell on the castle. Before going to sleep, it was time for Tomihime to carry out her end-of-day ritual.

She made a leisurely tour of the castle keep, surveying the scenery outside its windows. In the quietude of the deserted castle, the floorboards creaked distinctly beneath her feet. Deep down, Tomihime knew. This town, now sinking into darkness, glinting with the lights from the people's houses and the neon of downtown, belonged to her. This radiant white castle where she was now standing was who she was. This place was hers—indisputably, sickeningly, hers.

Inspiration for the Stories

"Smartening Up": *Musume Dōjōji (The Maid of Dōjō Temple)*—kabuki

For years Dōjō Temple has been without a bell. Legend has it that this was the doing of a young woman named Kiyohime, who fell in love with Anchin, a handsome priest at the temple. Being a priest, Anchin attempted to discourage Kiyohime's advances, and eventually, after countless rejections, Kiyohime's love morphed into a powerful hatred and she herself transformed into a fierce, fire-breathing serpent. The terrified priest ran to Dōjō Temple and hid beneath its huge bell. The snake coiled itself around the bell, breathing a stream of fire until the bell melted and the priest burned to death.

Ever since, Dōjō Temple not only has been bell-less, but its site has been off limits to women. The kabuki begins as the temple has finally been gifted with a new bell, for which a dedication ceremony is to be held. A beautiful young woman arrives at the temple, introducing herself as a traveling dancer named Hanako. Swayed by her enthusiasm and her beauty, the young monks agree to let her in the temple. Hanako steps inside the temple grounds and begins to dance at length. After a while the priests begin to suspect something is awry, but it is too late. By the time Hanako stands atop of the temple bell, she has revealed herself to be the spirit of Kiyohime.

"The Peony Lanterns": *Botan Dōrō* (*The Peony Lantern*)—rakugo

In the rakugo version of this well-known ghost story, Otsuyu meets Shinzaburō Hagiwara, a rōnin, or masterless samurai, and the two fall in love, but are forbidden from being together because they come from different social classes. So deep is Otsuyu's yearning that she eventually dies of lovesickness. Come Obon (the time in mid-August when spirits of the deceased return to earth), Otsuyu appears at Shinzaburō's door and the lovers enjoy a passionate reunion. Soon she is visiting him every night, bearing a peony lantern.

Noticing that Shinzaburō is growing more haggard and believing him to be possessed, his tenant hangs a talisman outside the door, preventing the entry of Otsuyu's ghost. Those passing the house at nightfall see a lantern floating sadly around the vicinity of Shinzaburō's house.

Eventually, the promise of financial compensation persuades the tenant and his wife to sell Shinzaburō's soul. They remove the talisman, and the lantern bobs joyfully inside. The next morning, Shinzaburō's corpse is found embracing a skeleton.

"My Superpower": *Yotsuya Kaidan* and *Kaidan Ichikawazutsumi*—rakugo

Yotsuya Kaidan is arguably the most famous Japanese ghost story of all time.

When Iemon's family decides that he should marry someone else, they send his wife Oiwa face cream laced with poison to disfigure her. Repulsed by Oiwa's transformed countenance, Iemon asks his brother Takuetsu to rape her to give him grounds for divorce; not having the heart to do so, Takuetsu instead shows Oiwa her own reflection. Oiwa flies into a rage, slips, and accidentally falls on her sword, later returning as a vengeful ghost.

Okon is an ex-geisha from another ghostly tale. She becomes friendly with the gambler Jirōkichi, and the two marry, although Jirōkichi's dissolute lifestyle means they never have any money. After a while, Okon develops a pimple on her face, which worsens into a terrible disease. Jirōkichi leaves to raise the money for her treatment, promising to return within ten days. He comes back on the eleventh day to find his wife gone. It is much later, when he has married another woman, that Okon returns to pay him a visit.

"Quite a Catch": *Kotsutsuri* (*Skeleton Fishing*)—rakugo
A male geisha is taken by a young gentleman on a boat trip down the river, along with various other entertainers. He isn't too keen to fish, but when his host offers a reward for whoever turns in the biggest catch, he applies himself, eventually fishing out a skeleton. He starts to throw it back into the river in disgust, but the host tells him to take it to a temple and have

it given rites. This he does, and returns home. In the early hours the following morning, he has a visitor in the form of a young woman. The woman tells him of her troubled past, and explains that she'd thrown herself into the river. Thanks to him, she says, she has been saved. When his neighbor comes to complain about the noise, the male geisha tells him what has happened, and the neighbor, wanting to find himself a woman, also manages to locate a skeleton. In the end, however, the ghost who comes to thank him is none other than the warlord Ishikawa Goemon, causing the neighbor great disappointment.

"The Jealous Type": *Neko no Tadanobu* (*Tadanobu the Cat*)—rakugo
One day, Jirōkichi, the pupil of a beautiful jōruri teacher, spies her drinking and snuggling up with a handsome married man, Tsunekichi. Filled with envy, Jirōkichi goes to tell the man's wife, Otowa, who is known for being "the jealous type." Sure enough, Otowa is seized by a fit of jealousy, making her want to rip her husband's kimono. But when Jirōkichi spurs her on to rip the kimono to shreds and smash the crockery, Otowa grows calm, and informs Jirōkichi that her husband is in the back room. Yet having just seen the scene of the

infidelity with his own eyes, Jirōkichi is unsatisfied, and eventually persuades Tsunekichi to go over to the teacher's house, where sure enough he finds another version of himself, drinking with the jōruri teacher. Eventually, it transpires that the man's double is in fact a cat. The cat's parents had been skinned alive and used to make the strings for a samisen, which is now kept in the jōruri teacher's house. Missing his parents, the cat would come along as Tsunekichi in order to meet them.

"Where the Wild Ladies Are"/"Loved One": *Hankonkō (Soul-Summoning Incense)*—rakugo
When a rōnin moves into a row of houses, he keeps his neighbors up by ringing a bell late into the night. When the steward goes over to complain, the rōnin explains that he is saying rites for his dead wife. He confesses that he has received soul-summoning incense from her, and that when he puts this on the fire and rings the bell, his wife appears before him. The steward asks the rōnin to demonstrate, which he does. The steward then asks for a little of the incense, so he, too, can meet his dead wife. But the rōnin refuses, despite all the steward's pleas, apologizing profusely and saying that this is one wish he cannot oblige.

Now seized by the longing to see his dead wife, the steward goes out and buys something that he thinks is soul-summoning incense, but which turns out to be medicine with a similar name. Back home, he throws it on the fire and waits. Finally he hears a knocking on the door and goes to answer it thinking it must be his wife, only to find someone coming to complain about all the smoke.

"A Fox's Life": *Tenjinyama (Mount Tenjin)*—rakugo
A rather peculiar man decides that, instead of having a cherry-blossom-viewing party under the trees like everyone else, he will go to the graveyard. Finishing up his solo banquet, he sees part of a skeleton sticking out of the earth, and takes it home. That night a beautiful woman appears to him, and ends up becoming his wife. When the man boasts to his neighbor about how cheap a ghost-wife is to maintain, the neighbor sets out to the temple find himself such a woman, but fails. He heads into the mountain and prays for a wife. On the way back he runs into a man holding a fox he has captured, and buys it off him. He then frees the fox, and again prays to be delivered a good wife. The fox transforms into a woman, chases after the man, and becomes his bride. Three years

after having a son, word of her true identity gets out and she runs away, leaving a verse on the shutters: "If you miss me, come to see me deep in the forests of Mount Tenjin in the south."

"What She Can Do": *Kosodate Yūrei* (*The Child-Raising Ghost*)—folk legend
One night, a pale-faced young woman knocks on the shutters of a candy shop, holding out a coin and asking for a sweet. The owner is suspicious, but relents and gives her one. This continues every night until, on the seventh night, the woman confesses to having no more money and instead offers to trade her haori jacket.

The next day, the shopkeeper leaves the jacket outside his shop. A rich man passing by recognizes the jacket as one that had been placed in the coffin of his daughter, buried just days before. When the shopkeeper explains the situation, the rich man rushes to his daughter's grave, from which he hears the cries of a baby. Digging up the coffin, he finds his daughter clutching a newborn. The six coins with which she had been buried, needed to cross the river into the other world, are gone, and instead the baby is sucking on candy. "You became a ghost to look after the child born in the grave!" exclaims the woman's father. "I promise to bring it up well in your stead." At this point, the woman's corpse drops its head as if to nod. The baby is taken in by the temple and grows up to be a great priest.

"Enoki": *Chibusa no Enoki (The Breast Tree)*—rakugo
With great cunning, the villain Sasashige muscles his way inside the house of Shigenobu and his devoted wife, Okise. Eventually Sasashige persuades the house servant to kill Shigenobu, and takes his place as Okise's husband. Next he orders the servant to kill Shigenobu and Okise's child, Mayotarō. The servant is about to throw the child into a river, but Shigenobu's ghost steps in and saves him. The servant decides to bring the child up in secret, surviving by living next to an enoki (Chinese hackberry), rumored to produce curative milk, in Akasaka-mura in the outskirts of Tokyo.

Meanwhile Okise has a child by Sasashige, but it dies. She develops growths on her breasts, which the enoki resin temporarily cures, but her dead husband comes to her in dreams, causing her more suffering. Sasashige attempts to let the pus in Okise's breasts by lancing them with his sword, but accidentally strikes her too deep, killing her. Sasashige goes mad and appears in Akasaka-mura where he is slayed by Mayotarō and Shigenobu's ghost.

"Silently Burning": *Yaoya Oshichi (Oshichi the Greengrocer's Daughter)*—folk legend

In Japan, every Buddhist temple and Shinto shrine has several unique woodcut stamps, or shuin. For a small fee, worshippers can have the temple or shrine calligrapher (often one of the monks or the kannushi) print these stamps in red ink on a piece of paper, and write the name of the temple, the day of the visit, and so on around the stamped portions. People often collect these stamps in purpose-made albums called shuinchō.

"A New Recruit": *Zashiki Warashi*—folk legend

The zashiki warashi is a much-loved member of the Japanese yōkai canon. A young child-spirit with a bowl cut, he or she usually takes up residence in zashiki—tatami-matted guest rooms. Although zashiki warashi have a reputation for being somewhat mischievous, they are also said to bring good luck to anyone who sees one, and to bestow fortune on the houses they reside in.

"Team Sarashina": *Momijigari* (*Maple Viewing*)—kabuki

The kabuki version of this story, adapted from the more classical Noh play, was the first ever motion picture to be made in Japan. Out hunting deer in the mountains, the warrior Taira no Koremochi stumbles across a beautiful woman and her retinue, enjoying a banquet to celebrate maple-leaf season. The warrior tries to ride past, but the woman bids him to drink with her. She turns out to be a demon-princess called Sarashina-hime. When the man falls into a drunken sleep, Sarashina-hime goes to abandon him and curses him to never awake, but a mountain god steps in and hands Koremochi a divine sword with which to defeat the demon-princess.

"A Day Off": *Shinobiyoru Koi wa Kusemono* (*The Suspicious Nighttime Visitor*)—kabuki

Mitsukuni, a young warrior, is exploring the ruined palace of Taira no Masakado when a sudden rainstorm forces him to take shelter in the palace, where he falls asleep. When he awakes, he finds beside him a mysterious and beautiful woman dressed like a courtesan, who confesses that she has been in love with him for a long time. Feeling suspicious, the young warrior tests her by narrating the story of Taira no Masakado's final hours on the battlefield. The woman is unable to hold back her tears, thus revealing her true identity as Masakado's daughter, Takiyasha no Hime. Seeing her attempt at seduction has failed, she instead asks Mitsukuni to break his allegiance to his clan and start a rebellion with her. Mitsukuni refuses and summons his warriors, but the princess easily defeats them with her magical powers, before disappearing and summoning an earthquake, from which Mitsukuni manages to escape. Finally, the princess reappears on top of a giant toad and unfurls Masakado's battle flag.

"Having a Blast": *San Nen Me (The Third Year)*—rakugo
In this tale, a dying woman makes an agreement with her husband that, should he be forced to remarry after her death, she will return to haunt him on his wedding night, thus scaring off his new bride. However, there is a hitch in the plan when she discovers she must wait three years for her hair, which has been shaved upon her death according to custom, to grow back. Without her fully grown hair, she reasons, she could not possibly be attractive to her husband.

By the time she finally appears as a ghost, her husband has given up on the idea of her ever returning, and he and his second wife have had a child.

"The Missing One": *Sarayashiki* (*Plate Mansion*)—
rakugo

This classic story tells of the beautiful Okiku, servant
to a samurai. For some time Okiku's master attempts
to have his way with Okiku, but she resists his advances. Growing impatient, the master tricks Okiku
into believing she has lost one of the household's
ten precious Delft plates. After counting the plates
over and over, Okiku finally breaks down in tears
to confess her oversight to her master, who agrees
to forgive her only if she will become his mistress.
When Okiku refuses, he throws her down a well to
her death.

Okiku's ghost, it is alleged, counts to nine before
emitting an ear-splitting screech. Successful exorcism
relies on a worldly being crying out a hearty "Ten!"
when she reaches the end of her count.

"On High": *Tenshu Monogatari* (*The Tale of the Castle
Keep*)—play

This play by Kyōka Izumi follows the story of spectral Tomihime gazing down from Himeji Castle keep,
where she resides with a retinue of female attendants,
at the dashing falconer Zushonosuke Himekawa.
When Tomihime uses her unearthly powers to

capture a falcon belonging to Himekawa's master to give to her sister Kamehime, the young Himekawa comes to the castle keep to reclaim it, and Himekawa and Tomihime fall in love.

Translator's Acknowledgments

I would like to thank Motoyuki Shibata for all his invaluable suggestions, as well as Meena Kandasamy, Saba Ahmed, and Yuka Igarashi, from whose thoughtful and creative edits the translation has benefitted hugely. And thanks above all to Aoko Matsuda, for writing a book that was such a delight to work on, and for being a continual inspiration to me.

AOKO MATSUDA is a writer and transla-
tor. In 2013, her debut book, *Stackable*, was nominated
for the Yukio Mishima Prize and the Noma Literary
New Face Prize. Her novella *The Girl Who Is Getting
Married* was published by Strangers Press in the UK
in 2016. In 2019, her short story "The Woman Dies"
was short-listed for a Shirley Jackson Award. She has
translated work by Karen Russell, Amelia Gray, and
Carmen Maria Machado into Japanese.

POLLY BARTON is a translator of Japanese
literature and nonfiction, currently based in Bristol,
UK. Her book-length translations include *Friendship
for Grown-Ups* by Nao-Cola Yamazaki, *Mikumari*
by Misumi Kubo, and *Spring Garden* by Tomoka
Shibasaki. She has translated short stories for *Words
Without Borders*, *The White Review*, and *Granta*. After
being awarded the 2019 Fitzcarraldo Editions Essay
Prize, she is currently working on a nonfiction book
entitled *Fifty Sounds*.